Kevin G

Cameron Banks
THE REALITY SHOW

B Global Entertainment, LLC.

2   Kevin Harrison
    Cameron Banks… The Reality Show

The sale of this book without its cover is unauthorized. If you purchased this book without a cover, you should be aware that it was reported to the publisher as "unsold and destroyed." Neither the author nor the publisher has received payment for the sale of this work in such case.

This story is strictly fictional. All of the characters and situations are based solely on the author's imagination, and not on real life people, circumstances, and events. Any situations in the book that resemble real life people, places, and events are strictly coincidence.

B Global Entertainment, LLC.
1562 N. Kenmar
Wichita, KS 67208
Copyright © 2007 by Kevin Harrison

Printed in the USA

ACKNOWLEDGEMENTS

    First of all, give an honor to God through whom all dreams and blessings are possible. No gift compares to the gift of life, so I owe you all the glory for allowing me to experience such a wonderful gift. I also want to thank my parents for supporting me in every endeavor (both practical and other) throughout this journey called life. Mom, thank you for stressing the importance of literacy and education. Dad, thank you for holding me accountable to become a man. I love you both dearly. To my daughter Ashley, thank you for inspiring me to pursue excellence. It is through your life that I am inspired to be my best, in hope that you are inspired to do the same. I hope and pray that my life has been a positive example. To Grandma Jones and to my late Grandma Harrison, thanks for the unconditional love and support throughout the years. To both late grandfathers, thanks for being additional role models, and thank you for continuing to watch over me while I try to "figure things out." To the ancestors... Thanks for enabling me to tap into positive and spiritual energy sources.

    To Michelle Chester and team at EMB Professional services – thank you so much for a wonderful job of re-editing the manuscript, and making it a much better read. To Mrs. Anita Guidry, thank you for the additional edits and feedback... as always, you have once again proven to be a rare and priceless jewel.

    Lastly, special thanks to the following people for helping make this project possible: Business partners – Riccardo Harris for reigniting me to get back after this dream, and Lady C for understanding (well – for sort of understanding – LOL) my occasional mood swings. To my only sibling Todd – 1 John 4:21 says "And this commandment we have from him. Whoever loves God, must also love his brother." We don't always see eye to eye, but I'm thankful for the unconditional love that we've

4   Kevin Harrison
    Cameron Banks… The Reality Show

always shared. Special thanks also to Ken Hawkins, Wendell Peete Jr., Bob and Pat Love, Marvin and Dorinda Lipscomb, Will Butler, The Holloway Family, Chez and the kids, and all of my cousins.

For anyone I may have neglected to mention, charge that to my mind and not my heart. It's not that I don't love you, but I may have overlooked you while rushing to make this deadline. I promise I won't leave you out of the next book in May.

K. Harrison

Let's skip the long preliminary –
I'm not your ordinary,
So called player, tryin'
to see you on the temporary
And I don't know you yet –
I know we just met
But every night's the first night for something –
I got something…

CHAPTER ONE
Office Politics

Every time I recall going against my father's advice, I also remember it coming back to haunt me. Nevertheless, in April of 2004, just months after my 31st birthday, I was once again about to go against one of dad's countless catch phrases…

"Son, never get your money and your pussy from the same place!!!" he used to tell me, and God knows I really tried to adhere to this rule. Unfortunately, this was a far easier thing to say than to do. This was especially the case on the day that I met Stacy Underhill.

I'm an accountant by trade, and at the time I was working as a CPA for Wallace, Underhill and Crabtree; the largest black owned accounting firm in Kansas. The Senior Partner and my direct boss, Mr. Underhill, had always spoken highly of his daughter Stacy, who had graduated from Stanford and was working for Price Waterhouse in Southern California. A desire to spend more time with family and a recent break up with her fiancé, as well as the obvious opportunity to make partner led Stacy back to Kansas where she accepted a position with daddy's company.

Although I had seen Stacy's pictures in Mr. Underhill's office before, I must admit, she was far more attractive in person. Her hair was like jet-black silk, and her butterscotch coated complexion carried the texture of flawless creamy caramel. She walked around with an air of confidence so dashing you'd think that she already owned the place. Her thick, full lips accentuated her perfectly straight teeth and adorable smile, and even though she wasn't just drop- dead gorgeous, she had a strong sense of sex appeal that immediately directed my attention towards her curvaceous hips and slender waistline.

"Banks, this is my daughter Stacy," Mr. Underhill stated boastfully. As I extended my hand towards Stacy, I couldn't help but to think of my buddy Reggie, who swears that a woman knows within the first 15 minutes of meeting a man, whether or not she is going to avoid him altogether, become his friend, fall in love with him... or just fuck him! I think it took Stacy about 15 seconds to figure this out with me. As our extended hands met and our eyes connected, a strange vibe took place between us that let me know almost immediately that she wanted to become more than just office buddies. I became so mesmerized by her sex appeal that I temporarily forgot that Mr. Underhill was standing there. My attention instantly shifted to her burgeoning cleavage; as my imagination drifted someplace outside of the office. I'm not sure how many times Mr. Underhill had called my name, but

I assume more than once or twice. By the time I snapped out of whatever zone I was in, his voice had become firm and aggressive as he demandingly shouted, "Banks... Are you okay? I asked you a question."

"I'm terribly sorry – sir," I replied to Mr. Underhill; sounding ridiculous as I blamed my absence of mind on my allergy medication. He then repeated his question. "Banks, I need you to put some of your other work on hold for a few days, so that you can spend time working with Stacy, introducing her to some of our larger clients, and just helping her get acclimated to how we do business here at Wallace, Underhill and Crabtree. Is that okay with you?"

Mr. Underhill was made man in every sense of the word, and therefore had no tolerance for excuses. Standing at only 5'6", his presence loomed more dominant and intimidating than any person I'd ever encountered. Tough life experiences and high expectations of others combined to produce an individual that most referred to simply as "one tough son of a bitch."

Mr. Underhill was an active black militant during the 60's Civil Rights movement, and witnessed many violent hate crimes as a child growing up in the racist South during the 50's. Plus, he was a Vietnam veteran who worked full-time during college in order to finance his own education. These are just a few of the many examples that have molded Mr. Underhill's no-

nonsense, zero tolerance for bullshit mentality. Therefore, I had no idea why he'd even ask for my approval of whether or not his request was okay with me. Whether it was okay or not, the only two acceptable answers to this or any other request from Mr. Underhill would be either yes or yes sir. Besides, I embraced the opportunity, as it would give me a chance to become better acquainted with Stacy, which is exactly what happened over the next few weeks.

Working closely with Stacy was quite the experience. Although I had originally viewed her as a spoiled little brat, riding Corporate America's fast track on the hem of daddy's coattail, the experience of us working together revealed to me that she was actually a very gifted accountant, who possessed a vast world of knowledge and experience. In other words, the chic really knew her shit! In fact, our level of professional respect for one another had grown so quickly, that my joy of working with her nearly began to outweigh my sexual desires for her. Then, one evening the two of us worked late on a very important project for Mr. Underhill. It was well past eight o'clock, so we decided to order pizza and work past midnight to ensure the project was completed by the deadline. I don't remember the exact time, but somewhere around midnight; as I approached the copy machine, Stacy gave me a look that was unlike any look she had given me before. I assumed this was just my imagination and I even tried to ignore it, but just as I thought I was in the clear, she walked over to the copy machine, bent down in front of me while grabbing my hands, and pulled my arms around her waist. Startled by her aggressive maneuver, I grew a bit nervous and uncertain of what to do next. Humored by my blatant uneasiness, she playfully whispered, "Relax baby, I don't bite." Her playful attitude helped settle my nerves as my attention immediately drifted towards her delicious looking, bowed legs. Her calves were muscular and athletically fit, and on her ankle a small tattoo posted the letters "WWJD"; a popular acronym posing the question, "What Would Jesus Do?" Oddly enough, of the several things I had on my mind to do to Stacy, I couldn't imagine any of my intentions being even remotely close to anything Jesus would ever consider.

By now, I'd become even more relaxed as my hands drifted from her waist to exploring various parts of her body, paying particular attention to her soft breasts and firm round ass. I leaned forward, placing my mouth gently on the back of her neck, allowing my tongue to softly massage her lower neck and shoulders while my left hand drifted slowly beneath her skirt. Carefully maneuvering, I gently slid her panties past her round, full hips down to her thighs. Then dropping to my knees, I positioned my mouth firmly around the soft satin material as I continued sliding her panties towards the floor with my mouth, until they surrounded her ankles in a manner similar to that of seductive cloth shackles in a porno film. Stacy lifted one foot at a time in order to assist me, as I continued using my mouth to finally slide her panties past her 2-inch heels and onto the floor.

Still positioned behind her, I gingerly began nibbling on her leg; starting at her ankle and moving slowly to her inner thigh just above the knees. The scent of her Issey Miyake perfume coupled with the smell of her natural womanhood drove me crazy, increasing my longing to taste her body in other places as well. Then I intentionally changed positions. Rolling onto my back, I grabbed Stacy's ankles for leverage, and then slid my head directly between her legs. Finally, I grabbed her by the waist, and slowly began pulling her towards the direction of my tongue. In a cat like fashion, her long and perfectly manicured fingernails clawed seductively along the contour of the copy machine, until she had knocked over a small bowl of mint candies that sat on a small table between the copier and drinking water dispenser. Finally, she placed both hands around my head, assuming a position that allowed for my tongue to easily explore the areas below her waist and between her thighs.

Stacy possessed a soft sweet taste, similar to that of cotton candy. Her plush inner-walls and pulsating clitoris had my adrenaline raging as I continued using my tongue to seek out her weak spot. Suddenly, a sweet sounding scream of passion escaped her lips, combining elements of crying, moaning and yelling to form the unique and indefinable word "Urrrrrrggghhhhh!!!" As this reprise continued several times, her voice and body began to quiver, indicating that her weak spot had been located. Knowing this, I began rapidly moving my tongue in circular motion repeatedly along Stacy's erogenous area until she ultimately could no longer tolerate my erotic presentation. She reached for my dark blue Hugo Boss sports coat and carefully placed it under my head, then thrust her pelvic area directly parallel to mine. She reached for one of the peppermints that had fallen to the floor and slowly un-wrapped it. Looking deeply into my eyes, she placed the peppermint in her mouth and started gently touching her tongue along my bottom lip, licking and sucking around my mouth while I began eagerly kicking off my shoes and sliding out of my dark blue trousers and boxer shorts. Her mouth remained active as she moved from my lips, down to my neck and chest area, simultaneously unbuttoning my dress shirt and tasting my body in one fluid motion. An erotic combination of seductive licking, suggestive sucking and tempting bites continued as she worked her way past my waist, finally placing her lips along the side of my shaft. Within seconds, her mouth had completely engulfed my manhood. Her warm, wet tongue moved like ocean waves along my tip as her lips managed to conduct a completely separate rhythm, gently sucking around the perimeter. Stacy moaned subtly, as the peppermint dissolved in her mouth, creating a cooling sensation that rippled throughout my body.

By now, I had become increasingly excited as I awaited the opportunity to penetrate Stacy's nearly naked body. Snatching her by her shoulder length hair, I pulled her face towards mine until our eyes connected. Then, as I looked deeply into her big brown eyes and gently stroked the side of her face, I licked my lips and softly uttered, "Damn!!! You are so fine!!!" Aroused by my compliment, she was now going wild - eagerly anticipating and desiring to feel my hardness penetrating inside of her. This sentiment was confirmed by frantic licking on my neck and shoulders; aggressive nibbling on my earlobes; and a combination of heavy breathing and high pitched moans. I spoke again, this time much more confident, commanding that she remove her blouse and brassiere. She quickly complied, then straddled herself over me, allowing me easy access to penetrate the walls of her private zone. Laying flat on my back, I began to exercise a series of pelvic movements, varying between inward and outward thrusts, and slow rhythmic gyrations. With her torso upright and her hands planted firmly against my chest, she began clawing her long fingernails into my flesh as sweat dripped from her eyebrows and a single teardrop fell from her left eye. I wiped the tear away with my index finger and gave her a very serious look as I kissed the tear away from my own finger. The teardrops continued to fall, so I reached around her neck, pulling her forward until she was lying flat on top of me. By now, a river of tears was falling from both eyes. One by one, I began kissing the tears off of her face while assuring her that everything would be alright. Eased by my comforting, her slow and calculated grinding motions from just moments ago were replaced by a vicious tirade of fast paced, rapid fire humping exhibitions as if she were about to reach her sexual climax. Once again, looking deeply into my eyes, Stacy gritted her teeth and repeatedly replied "Fuck me Cameron!!! Cameron, PLEASE FUCK ME!!!" Suddenly, the energy level of my body matched the aggressiveness of Stacy's motions, as our naked bodies remained intertwined - our behaviors emulating the lust of wild jungle animals.

Seconds later, the syncopation of her breathing had shifted. Her deep, full, and passionate breaths of air had become choppy lip quivering gasps. She appeared to hyperventilate. Stacy's heartbeat had shifted pace as well, causing her entire body to vibrate in a manner similar to that of a panic attack. Knowing that she was rapidly approaching the point of climax, I firmly pressed the palms of my hands flat against the back of her shoulders, pulling her body tightly towards mine. At that moment, her voice released a passionate scream of satisfaction. I could feel the warm wetness releasing rapidly from both our bodies, indicating that we'd arrived together.

The vision of our two sweat drenched bodies, lying on the floor, smiling and laughing together still seems as vivid as yesterday's sunlight. I can recall the moment with such clarity, that I even remember the insignificant details. Three dark colored sports jackets hung from the coat rack adjacent to Mr. Underhill's office door, an empty Doritos bag crumpled up on the floor lay beneath a plush leather office chair, and the old wicker ceiling fan above Stacy and I rotated in slow motion, casting a slight chill upon our unashamed nakedness.

They say in life that the same things that make you laugh eventually make you cry. At that very moment, the reality of such words escaped me, as Stacy and I lay naked on the carpet together. However, I would find these words to be very real in due time. So real, in fact that not only would I come to realize how tears and laughter co-exist; but also how that very moment would come back to haunt me immensely.

CHAPTER TWO
Back Then… They Didn't Want Me

During my undergraduate years at Kansas College, one face I remember vividly is that of Catherine Hightower. During school, the two of us were less than barely acquainted. In fact, I can't recall Cathy ever glancing in my direction. Truly a groupie for athletes and fraternity guys, she hardly knew I existed. Of course, later I'd wind up joining the greatest of all fraternities, but that's a completely different story. Anyway, to say that Cathy was a glutton for attention would be an understatement. Her name, face, and voice resonated across campus in a fashion as common as the changing of seasons or the passing of time. Through a series of calculative and deliberate efforts, Cathy would campaign with politician-like savvy in an effort to moisten her unquenchable thirst to be seen, heard, and perceived as a big shot. Although her efforts to cement her name as a permanent fixture on the campus social scene worked, I personally found her to be quite annoying. The untamed and scowling tonal quality of her voice created a discomfort comparable to the screeching of fingernails across a chalkboard.

Cathy's attire and accessories always remained fabulous though. Combine this with her affinity for lengthy hair weave, sea blue contacts lenses, and entirely too much facial make-up and she disguised her less than stellar outward appearance quite well. Her sagging cheekbones and sunken jaws revealed traits resembling those of an elderly lady rather than a 20 year old college student. To top all of this off, no curves whatsoever occupied her frail, 111 pound body, naturally drawing more attention to her long feet, bony ankles, and awkward build. Needless to say, I didn't think I'd ever in a million years become involved with Cathy, but as the old adage goes... Never say never – right?

It all started on Mother's Day Sunday in May of 2004. My parents belong to Greater Emmanuel Baptist Church, which is where I was baptized and my Christian faith groomed as a child. Lately though, I'd become more of a C.M.E than Baptist, since **C**hristmas, **M**other's Day, and **E**aster pretty much summed up the extent of my churchgoing. On this Mother's Day Sunday, Greater Emmanuel was conducting a joint service with another local church, and of course, my mother insisted that I attend.

As my parents and I entered through the dual doors and down the vestibule towards our seats, a heavy set, dark complexioned man named Deacon Burris joyously belted out the words to "The Lord Will Make a Way Somehow". What's funny is that even though I don't attend very often, it seems like every time that I am present; Brother Burris manages to be on program singing that same song.

Cameron Banks... The Reality Show

An assortment of colorful hats, large dangling earrings, and vibrant dress ties brilliantly complemented the sunlight that crept through the beautiful stained glass windows, filling the sanctuary with radiance similar to plaza lights during the holidays. Polite head nods and warm smiles greeted us as we ventured down the aisle towards the fourth pew from the front, finally taking our seats.

The young lady sitting in front of me turned her head slowly, curious as to who had been seated behind her. To my surprise, it was Cathy, who was currently residing in Kansas City where she worked in software sales. This particular weekend, she was in town visiting and had decided to accompany her parents to church. Cathy's appearance hadn't changed much since our college years, with the exception of a few minor subtleties, which made her slightly more attractive. Her thin, frail body still lacked definition, but she had filled out in a manner that accommodated her large feet and thin ankles, making them both appear less awkward. She wore a short, but very stylish haircut, with tapered sides and feathered top, which looked far more presentable than the ridiculous weave she had worn back in college. Finally, thank God, she had removed the blue contacts and was now more conservative and frugal with her application of make-up, which tended to minimize the aging quality of her facial features. By no means am I trying to paint the picture of a beauty queen, because that Cathy was not and never would be. However, her new look was at least presentable; unlike the almost 'creaturely' appearance she possessed in college.

    Though I never particularly cared much for Cathy, I exchanged a smile and a kind gesture in an effort to be cordial, figuring that this would be the extent of any and all interaction the two of us would share on this Mother's Day. How wrong was I for thinking such silliness!!! Immediately following service, Cathy followed me out to the parking lot in order to spark a conversation. For whatever reason, I guess Cathy felt the need to share her complete life story with me. Her divorce, the perils of her most recent relationship, and her career seemed to be the topics dominating the conversation. Perhaps, she recalled the two of us being better acquainted than we actually were, as she continued to share the intimate details of her life. Occasionally, she would pause and ask my opinion in between touchy feely gestures of hand grabbing, playful slaps on the shoulder, and lightly bumping me with her hip.

    Finally, my parents were approaching the parking lot, so Cathy and I brought our surprisingly pleasant conversation to an end. Reaching into her Coach purse, she fished around until finally pulling out a Blackberry and two of her business cards. As she handed me the cards, she gave a somewhat sensuous smile and in a friendly voice said, "Cameron, you should give me a call sometimes." I accepted both cards, placed them in my shirt pocket, and verbally stated my number as she fingered it into her Blackberry. The conversation ended, I gave Cathy an innocent hug, and we parted company, each going our separate ways alongside our parents.

From a distance, I'd always viewed Cathy as a vain, arrogant, and selfish individual with no compassion for anything other than money, material items, and an unparalleled desire to be perceived as some type of 'larger than life' figure. Honestly speaking, today's conversation was surprisingly enjoyable. In fact, I was exposed to a warmer and more approachable side of Cathy that I never thought previously existed. At that moment though, I still had no intention of ever calling Cathy, or any expectation of her calling me.

CHAPTER THREE
Meet the Parents

It was late May on a Saturday, and I was spending my evening at an elaborate dinner party hosted at the home of Mr. Underhill and his wife Delores. An all-star cast of high profile clients, important public figures, and scrutinizing family members made the bulk of the 'who's-who' guest list in attendance. Somehow, I managed to leave a charming impression on nearly everyone. This was particularly funny since I had no desire to be here as Stacy's beau. Now to me, a few steamy encounters meant nothing more than two individuals exploring one another sexually and just having some fun. I guess she looked at the situation differently, and even though no words were exchanged confirming any type of commitment, she had already taken the liberty of informing Mr. and Mrs. Underhill that the two of us had become seriously involved with one another. This was the very reason my attendance was requested here in the first place.

I guess I should've seen all of this coming. In fact, several signs had presented themselves throughout the week. For instance, Mr. Underhill referred to me as 'the son he never had' when introducing me to a group of new clients earlier in the week. What was more bizarre was that he had never previously inquired or discussed items of personal nature with me. Suddenly, he had become interested in my life outside of the workplace. This particular week, questions about my plans to get married, have children, and start a family became far more common than questions about my work. Still, none of this alarmed me until Friday of that week. That's when Underhill called me to his office and expressed the following words: "Cameron, I think you're a hell of an accountant and an even finer young man. Stacy told me all about the two of you and the wonderful relationship that you share; I want you to know that you certainly have my blessings son. I couldn't have asked for a better person to come into my daughter's life. She's been through a lot son, and I know that you won't hurt her. Anyway, we're having a dinner party at the house tomorrow evening and we'd love for you to join us. I'd like for you to meet my wife Delores and some of our other family members, and I'm sure Stacy would love to see you there as well. So what do you say son?"

Suddenly realizing that Stacy had presented me to her parents as her boyfriend, a sudden sense of queasiness had overtaken my stomach as my heart almost dropped to the floor. Of course, the two of us had shared some great times and even better sexual encounters. Most of our escapades were wild and without limitations, as we'd shared intimate experiences in places as common as our own homes and hotel rooms, to places as risky and spontaneous as on top of Mr. Underhill's desk after hours, the back of my Cadillac Escalade during drive-inn movies, the office conference room in the middle of the workday, and even in the ladies room of a fancy restaurant. To me though, this was nothing more than just sex. Wild, freaky and untamed sex of course, but still just sex nonetheless. Therefore, I have no idea how Stacy misconstrued what we shared to be a serious and meaningful relationship.

So, I found myself face to face with Mr. Underhill, unable to think of any possible way to correct his perception of my relationship with Stacy. For a split second, I actually contemplated telling him the truth as I searched for the politically correct way to inform him that his daughter and I were simply just fucking. I quickly came to my senses and opted against such foolishness while briefly casting a glance upon a series of photographs posted upon the bookshelf directly behind Mr. Underhill's head. One portrait in particular captured my eye and I zoomed in on the photo of Stacy and her proud father at her Stanford graduation. If it's true that a picture can tell a thousand words, then this picture could write a thesis on his passion for his only child. My eyes continued to wander, this time positioning upon the beautiful and expensive oak desk that occupied Mr. Underhill's immaculate office. I couldn't help but picture her naked, brown body sprawled wide and face down across this very desk just last week. I realized the immediate contrast between Mr. Underhill's fondest thoughts of Stacy compared with my graphic visual, and concluded that there was no safe way out of the situation. Whether I wanted to be in a relationship with Stacy or not, from that day forward I had to treat my situation with Stacy as such, in order to keep from potentially sabotaging my career. Therefore, I re-established eye contact with Mr. Underhill, reluctantly extended my hand towards his, gave him a solid and firm handshake, and replied, "Mr. Underhill, I'd love to attend your dinner party tomorrow evening."

So there I was, in attendance at the most extravagant and elaborate gala of galas. I must admit, the Underhill's estate was more than fabulous. Waterfalls cascading from rock gardens, man made ponds, and an Olympic-sized pool complemented the already illustrious landscape. An eloquently dressed string ensemble serenaded the premises, while other hired helpers assisted with serving, bartending, and distributing hors d'oeuvres. Serving tables decorated with ice sculptures and colorful fruit arrangements added elegance to splendid courtyards, surreal gardens, and well- groomed shrubbery. Plus, a multitude of important guests were decked out in ritzy gowns, sophisticated dinner jackets, and fabulous accessories.

Not to be outdone, I opted to dress in fashionable black for this evening's function. For starters, a solid black Joseph

Abboud formal suit and Black Canali slip-ons were the highlights of my attire. My shirt, which was of course tailor-made, showcased oversized French cuffs and hidden lapel buttons. The black face Movado strapped to my wrist added an additional spark of dark curiosity to my already mysterious and elegant ensemble. Finally, a set of oil black cuff links and a smoke black Italian-made tie provided the polishing final touches to my presentation. To ensure that my scent possessed a sense of appeal equal to the mysterious 'blackness' of my visual display, my theme was completed by my choice of colognes for tonight's affair - a fragrance simply called BLACK, by Kenneth Cole.

Now I'm far from being a vain person, and certainly not conceited. In all honesty though, the only way I could've been any more dressed to kill is if I'd been wearing an O.J. Simpson jersey, or a Freddy Krueger mask.

Meanwhile, Stacy and her parents were busy parading me around as if I was some type of science exhibit or show-n-tell project. Relatives and friends alike anxiously awaited the opportunity to meet 'Stacy's man' as I continued leveraging a fake smile and an Emmy caliber performance that even Sidney Poitier would envy. Throughout the night, I demonstrated precise and flawless execution as I answered flurries of questions and responded to countless statements pertaining to me and Stacy.

"How long have the two of you been together?"

"Do we hear wedding bells?"

"I bet you two would have beautiful children."

"It's wonderful that the two of you love each other."

These particular remarks seemed to rank among the most common items of curiosity, as the Underhill social gala was rapidly turning into 'Something about Cameron'. Of course, the funniest thing I heard all night was Stacy's grandmother lecturing me on waiting until after we're married to become sexually active. Poor old lady actually thought that Stacy was a virgin --- bless her heart. Based on my experiences with Stacy, I'd be willing to bet that her lust demons never saw a dull moment during her undergraduate years at Stanford.

Finally unable to tolerate being on display much longer, I excused myself for the restroom with the intention of losing myself in the crowd. As I ventured away, my cellular phone rang with a familiar number appearing on the caller-id, but I didn't recognize it right away. I finally answered and was greeted by the very friendly voice of Ms. Cheyenne Brown.

Cheyenne (or Shy as I sometimes called her) and I went back quite a ways, and although the two of us were never truly compatible, we'll always share a strange type of respect for one another.

Without question, I loved Shy, but the two of us came from such different worlds that trying to have a relationship would result in an inevitable train wreck.

Since I'd now become the man of the hour at the Underhill social function, I knew I wouldn't be able to speak with her for long, so I quickly exchanged brief words of small talk and hurried off the phone, promising to call her the next morning.

Suddenly, from the side of the house, Stacy seemingly appeared from almost nowhere and immediately asked who I was on the phone with. I lied and said that it was my boy Reggie, but she knew better. After all, she'd obviously been keeping a tab on me from the moment I excused myself from her and her parents just 10 minutes prior. The two of us went back and forth and eventually got a bit loud. I begged Stacy not to make a scene at the dinner party, but she continued to raise her voice at me. Pretty soon, Stacy requested to look at my call register, but I refused to allow this. She began cursing and calling me everything from "no good motherfuckers" to "sorry punk ass cheating bastards" and everything else ungodly that you can imagine calling a person. A few heads started to turn in our direction as I continued trying to keep Stacy cool and level headed.

"Stacy, this is your mom and dad's party. We can't be acting like this. Come on now baby, this is embarrassing to us and to them!" I replied desperately.

My commentary ceased to move Stacy, as she sharply responded saying, "Nigga I wouldn't give a fuck! You think you can play me like I'm some dumb ass bitch. Who the fuck was that on the phone Cameron?"

I was beginning to get uneasy as the scene started to escalate into something that could've potentially made a mockery of the whole party. Thinking quickly, I requested to that we step inside the house in order to continue this conversation in private. Angrily agreeing to this, she grabbed me by my arm, and in a vicious manner, pulled me through the threshold of two large glass French style patio doors. Fortunately, only a small handful of Mr. Underhill's distinguished visitors witnessed the small altercation between she and I, and we were able to escape before anything unfixable were to take place.

She then briskly led me through the kitchen, down a hallway, up a spiral staircase, and into a moderate sized bathroom. She pulled me into the bathroom, closing and locking the door behind us. By this time, she was crying profusely and angrily pushed me down onto the toilet seat, fell to her knees and began beating me in the chest with a flurry of open hands, balled fists, and fingernail clawing swipes. This entire time, she continued crying, yelling and calling me names that I won't dare repeat.

Suddenly, her fingers gently slid from my chest area towards my stomach. The violent and aggressive demonstration of hands from just moments earlier had casually shifted into a subtle and easy stroking maneuver. Stacy continued stroking my body with care as she moved past my stomach and down towards my waist. Although she was still crying, her tears casually transitioned from the unpredictable rage of white water rapids to the seductive essence of slow motion raindrops.

Before I knew it, a sense of placid serenity had overtaken Stacy as her head was now utilizing my lap as a comfortable resting place. Her hair slightly draped my leg as my slacks absorbed her tears, which had subsided, becoming motionless. She moved her hand carefully from my waste to my zipper, but didn't immediately make an attempt to unfasten my trousers. Instead, she allowed her long elegant nails and flawless smooth fingers to passionately massage through my clothes, exciting me to the point that a bulging sensation occurred. With her head still lying in my lap, Stacy unzipped my trousers and in a deliberate fashion, navigated her hand through the threshold until I gently felt the sensation of her fingers and nails softly stroking the contour of my copulatory organ. Eager to assist, I begin to calmly stroke the top of Stacy's head with one hand while helping her unfasten my belt with the other until my trousers were wide open, giving her uninhibited access to freely taste and explore my masculinity. I made an attempt to stand up in order to better position myself to penetrate Stacy from behind, but she gave me a firm push and I abruptly reassumed my position on the toilet seat. Stacy abruptly wrapped both hands around my phallus until her fingers were interlocked. She shifted the direction of her head until our eyes were in direct contact. With motionless tears still occupying her face, she looked at me and in a whimpering voice says - "Cameron - I love you." - "I love you sooooo much." - "I don't ever want to lose you." – "I can't lose you."

Stacy's head reassumed its position on my lap as one of her hands slid down the side of my leg until becoming firmly wrapped around my ankle. With the other hand still caressing my erection, Stacy's mouth slowly and passionately consumed me. Pleasing me orally had become a very common affair for Stacy, but this moment felt entirely different than previous encounters. Her tongue moved circularly and slowly, causing a pulsating sensation to develop. The rhythm of her mouth was steady, seeming to almost deliberately match pace with my heartbeat and throbbing erection. As she continued to taste me, her fury and rage continued to dissipate as her tears completely dissolved. She now seemingly had found placidity similar to that which accommodates an infant when given a pacifier or being breast-fed. As her mouth continued to soothe me, I realized that nothing in the world could have made Stacy more content than this very moment. This episode continued for the next 30 minutes or so. Suddenly, a tingling sensation had completely overtaken every dimension of my partially disrobed body. The combined feeling of anticipation and energy seemed to slowly move through me from each direction until ultimately merging to form what felt like an expanded balloon that had surpassed its capacity for helium. Stacy continued pleasing me orally as the anticipation of a sensual explosion continued fertilizing the soils of my amorous imagination.

My body became firm and rigid as my hands and feet suddenly developed a sense of shakiness. I moved both hands around Stacy's head and began firmly massaging her scalp with my fingertips as I boldly pulled her face tightly towards my body, allowing her long wild hair to freely drape over my stomach. The raging energy inside of me finally exploded in the form of a joyous and passionate outburst. Stacy became excited as she eagerly consumed each drop of flowing affection released from my weakening body. My tension slowly eased as my tightly clinched torso expanded and my stiffened muscles became suddenly relaxed. Stacy lifted her head, and looked deeply into my eyes once again. With a look of despair in her face, she uttered "I love you Cameron."

Uneasy about this entire scenario, I became cautious not to incite another one of Stacy's neurotic mood swings. Endless moments of silence occupied the space between us as our eyes remained locked; she anxiously awaited my response. Although I had yet to truly get to know her, this particular evening revealed startling traits about her character. For starters, she was a jealous and possessive individual who couldn't differentiate sex from love. Even though the bulk of our encounters consisted of her seducing me, and I had never spoken of love in conversations with Stacy; she was still sadly under the impression that our exchanges of physical intimacy represented a mutual exchange of love. What's even more disheartening was that this wasn't the first time, nor would it be the last that she would resort to sexual behaviors as a solution for resolving conflict. Physically pleasing the men she's loved has obviously been her warped method of dealing with her relationship concerns. This dysfunctional behavior would become far too common in the days to come, as my dishonesty with Stacy would continue to fuel these potentially dangerous fires.

Taking all of this into account, I realized I was running out of time as she awaited a response to her "I love you" from what had now had been about a minute ago. I swallowed, licked my lips and took a deep breath before attempting to say a word. I then softly caressed the side of her face to buy time, while rehearsing my words silently to myself. Her expression told me that she was becoming impatient, so I cleared my throat one last time as I prepared to speak. I was fully aware of the fact that I didn't love her and this entire episode had me wondering whether or not I even still liked her. I was also aware of the potential dangers that could derive from misleading her. Nevertheless, I opted for what seemed to be the easy way out and allowed the words "I love you too Stacy" to roll off my tongue effortlessly. Surprised by my own ability to be so cold hearted, I realized that expressing such words and not meaning them couldn't have been an easier task. I honestly felt no remorse for such selfish and asinine behavior, as my immediate mission had been accomplished. Stacy was now content and elated by my false display of emotion.

Continuing to further trap myself in this lie, I repeated the words over several times until almost believing them myself as my voice sounded more expressive and sincere each time I spoke… "I love you, I do… I love you Stacy!" Finally, I grabbed her face tightly and turned her eyes towards mine as my voice became even more intense. "Do you hear me Stacy? I ain't going no where… I LOVE YOU."

After several minutes of clinging to me tightly and crying in my arms; our dramatic scene finally came to a close. The two of us adjusted our attire and prepared to rejoin the dinner party. As we exited the bathroom together and gradually approached the staircase that led us back into the courtyard, I looked at Stacy and silently asked myself if I could ever really grow to love her. Previously, the answer would have simply been "no". But after this outrageous behavior, the answer had certainly escalated to "Hell No!"

We finally returned to the courtyard together and resumed entertaining the countless distinguished guests, creating the illusion that we'd never parted. Side by side, hand in hand, and with smiles on our faces, this night would become just one of many moments that I would play out this very dangerous role while living this even more dangerous lie. This night would eventually go done in history as one of many nights that I'd certainly live to regret!

CHAPTER FOUR
Ghetto Heaven

Tonight's the night
Everything will be alright
There's no need to be uptight
Ghettos of the world unite...

It was Sunday morning, the day after the Underhill's dinner affair. You'd think I would've slept in late after the combination of the previous night's drama and several glasses of Hendrix Gin. However, I got up at around 7:00 a.m. without experiencing even the slightest of hangovers. At 7:45 a.m. I went on a two mile run with my personal trainer. I returned home at nine and decided to give Cheyenne a call.

I dialed the number and four long rings were finally interrupted by a harsh yet alluring voice that simply said, "Hello". I was typically accustomed to less traditional greetings when calling her, so I was slightly thrown off. I guess I expected more of a "Yo - what up?" or a "Holla at your girl", or something to that effect rather than a typical hello response. Hearing her voice ignited pleasant sensations. I've always adored Cheyenne Brown, so the time we'd spent apart had seemed as endless to me as the very space between the earth and the stars. I certainly missed her and I eagerly embraced the opportunity of us becoming reacquainted.

After a few moments of small talk and playing catch up, Cheyenne extended an invitation for me to visit her later in the afternoon. I eagerly accepted the invitation, promising that I'd arrive at 2:00. We continued to laugh and talk for a while, until I received a call registering 'private' coming in on the other line. I clicked over and discovered that it was Stacy. I had no idea why she called me private, but I'm sure her jealous intuition had made her suspicious, so I didn't even bother clicking back over to Cheyenne, hoping that Stacy would fail to discover that I'd been on the phone.

Of course, the first thing out of her mouth was, "Who are you on the phone with?" and, "Why'd it take you so long to answer?" Without hesitating, I once again lied on Reggie. Using Reg as my scapegoat was becoming so common that before all is said and done, Stacy was gonna hate his black ass.

"Stacy you remember me telling you about Reggie Mitchell, don't you? My partner that lives in Dallas? The stockbroker."

I could tell that she wasn't really buying this, but her jealous suspicions took a backseat to her real reason for calling. She changed the subject in order to invite me to her parent's home for a late lunch between two and two-thirty. Now it's obvious that I can't be in two places at once, but I also realized the potential danger in saying 'no. In order to think of what to say next, I bought myself a brief moment by asking a question.

"Baby, how long do you plan on visiting your parents?"

She paused for a split second, then replied - "I don't know, probably a few hours, why?

Her six-second response was all the time I needed to become poised and ready to deliver my reply.

"I'd love to join you and your parents for lunch, but here's the deal. Dad is working on one of his rental properties today and I promised I'd help him out for a little while. We won't be through until around four, so why don't you go ahead and I'll come by after four if you're still there"

Over the years, I'd perfected lying to an art form, so I immediately realized that my story was less than solid and contained a multitude of vulnerabilities. I expected her to attack me with questions pertaining to the address of the home we'd be working on, or even offering to work with us. But Stacy, obviously pre-occupied by something else, opted to let me off the hook easy.

"Okay Cameron, just come by when you finish."

We exchanged "I love you" and brought our conversation to a peaceful ending. I was suddenly overtaken by the sense of relief in knowing that I could still meet my 2:00 obligation with

Cheyenne without disappointing Stacy. The last thing I wanted to do was incite another of Stacy's neurotic outbreaks.

I lived on the far west side of town, so I had an approximate 15 minute drive to get to Cheyenne's home, which was on the northeast side. I left my home at 1:45 p.m. and when 2:00 finally arrived, I was approaching Cheyenne's residence right on time. On one side of her home, the neighbors had an old refrigerator and two philodendrons' in huge flower pots sitting on the porch. The house on the other side was boarded up and abandoned. Her younger brother Jamal was seated on the steps or her home, drinking a can of Colt 45 while a young lady in her early 20's busily braided his hair. At the end of the block sat a strip mall that housed an Asian owned store called "Keepin' Kute" where everything from black hair care products to knock-off designer jeans could be purchased. Believe it or not, a COGIC Church and a liquor store actually occupy space in the very same mall.

Cheyenne's quaint and well-kept home appeared almost out of place, sharing the street with several condemned and run down properties. Gang insignia painted on the side of several walls and conspicuous behavior represented obvious illegal activity. From the outside looking in, I'm sure I appeared to be completely out of my element as I got out of my 740 BMW and approached the front door to Cheyenne's home. My precise haircut, cleanly shaven face, wire- framed glasses and white oxford shirt probably don't paint the stereotype of a person who found this to be a comfortable environment. For the record though, I grew up in this hood and still visited on a frequent basis. Some of my closest friends lived there, plus I just liked keeping in perspective where I came from. Honestly speaking, I'm more relaxed in the hood than I've ever been at functions like the Underhill's elaborate little dinner soirée.

As I approached the front porch, Jamal took a huge gulp of his malt liquor then pointed towards the door. In a raspy voice, he mumbled "Gone on in man. She in da house!!"

I walked around Jamal and his hairstyling female friend, calmly opened the front door and entered through the living room. The combined fragrance of burning incense, marijuana, and Victoria's Secret Body Lotion filled the air, creating an aroma that invoked sensations of both mystery and seduction. Shy was seated on the couch next to another young lady I'd never met. Directly in front of them, a *"Sister to Sister"* magazine, a box of Swisher Sweet cigars, and a small bag of bud trees sat on top of a black lacquered coffee table. An oversized painting of a black panther in a shiny brass frame hung on the wall behind them. Shy's friend never looked up, as the task of removing the tobacco from one of the cigars had her completely occupied for the moment. I attempted to speak to Cheyenne, but the competing volumes of both 106 & Park on the television and Snoop on the CD player submerged the sound of my voice.

Seemingly excited to see me, Cheyenne lifted herself from the couch and walked towards me. In a manner that seemed almost intentional, she continued moving in my direction, positioning her enormous cleavage in direct alignment with my visual path. Although artificial, her hairstyle was also enticing. The sides were tapered and short, with linear wave patters held in place by stiff gel pomade. The waves slowly dissipated into thicker hair towards the middle of the head until finally completely dissolving into a feathery body of store bought weave, styled with full round curls rolling forward in a manner resembling ocean tides. Finally, blonde and burgundy streaks accentuated by sparse dashes of sparkling glitter provided the illusion of shiny platinum raindrops and multi-colored waterfalls showering her subtle beige complexion. Her attire consisted of a yellow mid-drift t-shirt reading "World Class Bitch" across her breasts and a pair of skin-tight jean shorts that barely contained her full hips and solid round posterior.

Cheyenne's aura truly encompassed the stereotypical images that most would categorize derogatorily with names such as 'hood rat' or 'chicken head'. Much like the calming sensation of the rivers reflection or the soothing spirit of a gentle breeze, I've always viewed her as more of a priceless and intangible sentiment. Regardless of how she'd been perceived by everyone else, she would always be a precious jewel to me.

The two of us hadn't been in touch in quite some time, so a sense of uneasiness consumed me as she drew near. I pondered possible outcomes of the encounter at hand. While thinking to myself that perhaps a handshake would show far too little affection, I decided that a kiss would show too much. Sensing my uncertainty, she took matters into her own hands and gave me a huge hug. Now typically a hug is an innocent gesture, but this certainly wasn't the type of hug you share at a family reunion. She planted her hands firmly against my back, as she used her fingers to massage my shoulders in a manner that was both alluring and seductive. Her body felt warm and extremely inviting, and she occasionally pulled me towards her as if to intentionally feel the throbbing bulge below my waist. Still naïve to all of this, her next series of actions made the presence of both her sexual desires and intentions abundantly clear. Her hands moved from my shoulders and back briskly down the direction of my waistline. She pulled me towards her, this time much tighter than a few moments ago. Ignoring the fact that another person was in the room, she dispersed a slight grinding motion while fixating her lips closely against my ear and whispering, "Cameron, you know I missed this baby... don't you?"

By this time, I was aroused but still a bit uncomfortable with the whole situation. I definitely didn't love Stacy Underhill, but the consequences of cheating on her with Cheyenne terrified me tremendously. On the other hand, I possessed serious feelings for Cheyenne, but trusting her to be discreet would be the equivalent of trusting a used car salesman at the end of the month. Besides, our worlds were as different as laughter and tears. Perhaps deep down, Cheyenne was much more my type than the high-post, educated divas I'd become accustomed to. At the same time though, status, education, and perception had forced me into playing the role of a character that others expected to see with such types. Sadly enough, I had played the part of this character so well that I often lost sight of my own true identity as well as what I truly seek in a mate. Could it be that my constant quest for greener pastures had caused me to overlook true love in Cheyenne? Could it be that Cheyenne was indeed my true soul mate?

After several moments of aimless daydreaming, Cheyenne's phone rang. Her behavior changed drastically once she answered the phone. Her reaction to the voice on the line dictated characteristics of both nervous energy and bitter frustration. Realizing that the call was from no one other than K-9 (Canine), I suddenly snapped out of my romantic incubus and reminded myself of all of the drama that Cheyenne has put me through over the years because of K-9.

K-9's real name is Keldwin Stevens III. With such a wholesome and respectable sounding name, I assume his folks had aspirations of him someday becoming a lawyer, doctor, or something distinguished and respectable. Instead, K-9 decided to invest all of his energy, talent, and effort into becoming a complete asshole, and I must say - he's done so with a huge degree of success. Standing at about 6'1", K-9's skin complexion is as dark as midnight and his facial features resemble those of an angry pit bull. A huge pug nose takes center stage, complimented by beady eyes, bad skin, and a rapidly receding hairline. I typically don't speak badly about people, but this was indeed one of the ugliest niggas I've ever laid eyes on. A professional drug dealer by trade, K-9 had somehow developed the reputation on the streets as being some type of hardcore, tough ass gangster. I won't go into great detail about the altercations he and I have had, but I will say this... even if no one else ever knew the truth about K-9, he and I both know that deep down, he's as soft as cotton with the heart of a goldfish.

I'm not sure if Shy considered K-9 her boyfriend or what the relationship was between them, but when she and I first became involved, she made it quite clear that no matter what, she was never going to discontinue her relationship with K-9.

Although this was over a year ago, I recalled her words as if she had just spoken them today.

"Cameron, I like you a lot and I want to see you, but I can't and ain't gone NEVER quit fuckin' with K-9. That's just the way it's gone be!"

It's strange to me that she would sell herself out at such a paltry price. Despite the fact that she's 100% hood, she was actually a pretty intelligent chic, but absolutely dumb when it comes to dealing with this lowlife piece of shit. The poor child had gone above and beyond in doing ANYTHING and EVERYTHING to please K-9 and for nothing more than a few small material perks. Since I personally had never gotten this love thing figured out myself, I'd be quite the hypocrite to attack someone else's perception of such a tender and ambivalent emotion. Nevertheless, I found difficulty in visualizing how paying someone's rent, supporting their habits, and providing for their cosmetic upkeep could ever equate to love.

K-9's physical and mental abusiveness towards Shy was something that I was also well aware of. Somehow though, the long walks, dinner dates, intimate conversations, and cultural experiences that I'd shared with her had always taken a backseat to K-9's willingness to toss out a few dollars from time to time, humiliate her publicly, and constantly degrade her.

I'm uncertain as to why, but she seemed to find fascination in the lifestyles of pimps, players, and street hustlers. Maybe it's the fact that her father and uncle once monopolized every illegal enterprise that transpired on the North side. Perhaps she's still star struck by images similar to those portrayed by characters such as Nino Brown in *New Jack City* or Priest in *Super Fly*. Maybe that lifestyle was all she'd truly ever know. For whatever reason, she remained engaged in a continual quest to satisfy her undeniable and insatiable hunger for ghetto folklore. She found her relationship with K-9 both a gratifying and accommodating fix, satisfying this bitter and destructive appetite.

Though truly an unhealthy situation, Cheyenne had somehow allowed herself to perceive this valueless pattern as something containing fruitful and rewarding purpose for her life. In actuality though, her laughter and boisterous demeanor seemed to me like nothing more than an empty façade that masked her obvious unhappiness.

After approximately 10 minutes, Cheyenne ended her phone conversation with K-9. At first I wasn't totally sure why, but her attitude had changed drastically. Her previous touchy-feely vibe from earlier had become cold, distant, and bitter. The pleasant and flirtatious smile on her face had shifted into becoming a blank and motionless stare. Though she tried to restrain them, countless teardrops began melting down her warm cheeks in a manner resembling the icicles that defrost from frozen Kansas Maplewood trees as winter makes way for the entry of springtime.

It's obvious that K-9 had delivered extremely harsh words to Cheyenne and it had just occurred to me why! Apparently he had driven by the house and saw my car parked outside. This had happened on one previous occasion that resulted in a small physical altercation between the two of us. Now, I'm certainly not claiming to be some bad ass tough guy, but I'm also not to be taken lightly just because my lifestyle and dress depict the part of a corporate intellectual square. All in all, I definitely hate physical altercations, but this particular incident ended with K-9 flat on his back. I often wonder why he never came back with his cronies seeking revenge. Of course, a person with his street cred would've had a hell of a time justifying getting his ass whipped by a CPA or even needing help for such a situation. Therefore, I guess he figured the best bet would be to just ignore me and pretend the situation never happened. Taking all these things into consideration, I guess he decided that this day wouldn't be a good day to once again be fooled by the designer suits and choirboy image.

With tears still in her eyes, Cheyenne's trembling voice softly spoke.

"Cameron, K-9 is outside in the car trippin" she said, with a look of frustration on her face and her hand covering her forehead.

The fear and discomfort I detected in her voice revealed that I should probably be leaving, so the conversation ended abruptly and I headed towards the front door.

Aroused and excited best explain my feelings after our slight exchange of bodily contact and brief small talk. The encounter spawned memories of the many wild, uninhibited, and lust filled exchanges the two of us once shared, thus strengthening my desire for us to once again resume spending time alone with one another. Before I left, I asked about her availability for the upcoming Friday. She agreed to a Friday night rendezvous and promised that getting away from K-9 wouldn't be an issue. Finally, we said our goodbyes and I exited the front door.

I walked outside, and sure enough there was K-9, parked along the curb in his black and chrome 600 Mercedes Sports coupe. As I approached my vehicle, I guess my ornery side came out. I deliberately turned my head in the direction of K-9 in order to ensure that my smirking face and swaggering walk were visible. Once I was certain that eye contact was established, I began nodding my head in an arrogant and taunting fashion. Obviously pissed off, he responded with an evil, menacing grimace, but remained seated in his vehicle until I had entered the car and closed the door behind me.

As I drove away, I guess curiosity got the best of me. My attention was fixed on the domestic dispute occurring on Cheyenne's front porch. Finally, the reflection of pushing, arguing, and cussing slowly dissipated until completely dissolving from my rearview mirror. I would've liked to have stayed and defended her, but whatever they needed to discuss didn't concern me. I just hoped and prayed that she'd be okay.

I departed at three, so I had plenty of time to make it to Stacy's parent's home by four o'clock. I figured I'd even surprise her by arriving early. I called and informed her that I was en route, and I headed to the Underhill's home where I concluded my day in a rather uneventful fashion.

CHAPTER FIVE
White Chic's

The next day at work was uneventful other than the fact that Stacy's vibe was somewhat cold and uninviting. I tried to spark up several conversations with her, but her demeanor remained standoffish and even unpleasant. I went as far as asking her how she was feeling and whether or not things were okay, but the only reciprocating responses I could get were a series of short, cold, and emotionless one line remarks, accompanied by shoulder shrugs, twisted lips, and sharp cutting eyes. I'm sure she had no clue of my brief visit with Cheyenne yesterday, but it was obvious that her keen intuition had alerted her something wasn't quite right.

Finally five o'clock arrived and the seemingly longest workday ever had come to an end. I left the office immediately en route towards the parking lot, jumped into my car, and headed home. Though Kansas driving typically presents rather boring scenery, I must admit it to be far more relaxing and pleasant than those rush hour drives I experienced while residing in Houston and Atlanta. Typically, I can get anywhere in Wichita in about 15 minutes or less. The drive home from work, even on the busiest days may take about 10 minutes, so although the nightlife tends to be a bit bland around here, I can definitely say that I don't miss the bumper to bumper traffic and road rage that comes with bigger cities.

As I pulled into my garage, my cell phone rang. The caller-id screen boldly displayed *"private,"* so I knew that it was no one other than Stacy attempting to be inconspicuous. It had become common practice for her to call me "private" whenever she was angry or disappointed with me. I suppose she convinced herself that I wouldn't know it was her, even though this had become quite the familiar pattern. I was somewhat exhausted, so I didn't even bother answering. Besides, she didn't have much to say to me at work all day, so why the hell did she desire to bother me now.

I entered my kitchen through the garage and fixed myself a glass of cognac. Then, I plopped my fatigued body onto the living room couch and took a moment to collect my thoughts. Extreme mismanagement of both my professional and personal life was starting to take toll on me, and lately I had been really stressing out.

My workload was becoming more than challenging, and personal drama was causing me to fall further behind on several deadlines that needed to be met. My inability to say "NO" to Mr. Underhill didn't help my situation much. Just recently he had handed me the account of perhaps his wealthiest and most important client; an older white gentleman named Robin

Wilkens. I met Wilkens and his daughter Janie at the Underhill dinner party last week, where he and I conversed about everything from sports and hobbies to politics and finance. Apparently, he was impressed by our initial encounter, and had requested that I serve as the principle on all of his accounts.

I realized the extreme significance of getting caught up on my workload, but I definitely didn't look forward to the tedious evenings and weekends that such a task would require. Although my professional reputation and even my very employment depended upon me continuing to deliver high quality work, I still struggled to find the inspiration to make such a commitment. Besides, I definitely wasn't working the upcoming Friday evening. I had a date planned with Cheyenne that I eagerly looked forward to.

Still relaxing on the couch, I continued thinking about my life and each of its dramatic interpretations. My eyes remain fixated on the blank wall in front of me, while I became totally abducted by the wide variety of thoughts suddenly occupying my utterly disturbed mind. Other than taking occasional sips from my cognac glass, I remained on the couch practically motionless as I pondered what the future had in store for me. Would I ever get my workload caught up? How would I manage to disappear with Cheyenne without Stacy getting suspicious? What questions would Stacy ask? What lies would I tell? These, among many other questions, continued to dominate my mental space, until I finally finished my drink and fell asleep on the couch.

A couple of hours passed and I was suddenly and abruptly awakened by the annoying sound of my cellular phone ringing. I was certain that this was no one other than Stacy, so without even checking the display screen, I quickly sat up and answered in an attempt to accommodate Stacy in a manner that would hopefully prevent a surprise visit.

"WHAT!" I blurted out in a rather rude and abrasive voice; preparing myself for what I was sure was about to be a verbal altercation with Stacy.

To my surprise, it wasn't her on the other line after all. In fact, I didn't have a clue exactly who this mystery voice belonged to. Startled by the unpleasant nature of my initial greeting, the female voice on the other line disturbingly replied - "Oookay, maybe I picked a bad time to bother you. I can call back some other time."

Suddenly embarrassed by my behavior, I apologized and politely asked who I was speaking with. To my surprise, it was Janie Wilkens; someone who I never expected a call from. Other than the exchange of a cordial "pleasure to meet you" at the Underhill dinner party, Janie and I had never exchanged words. Why on earth would she be calling me? I wondered.

"Hey Cameron, this is Janie Wilkens. My father and I met you at the Underhill's house party. Do you remember meeting me?" Reluctantly, I replied with a very passive, "sure, I remember", while I remained perplexed as to the reason for her call.

"I hate to bother you and I hope that you don't find this call inappropriate, but I borrowed your number from my dad's rolodex. I wanted to say more to you at the dinner affair the other night, but Stacy and her parents never seemed to give you much breathing room."

Our conversation started at 9:15 p.m. and we continued talking to one another until close to midnight. Janie was definitely a spoiled little rich girl who was accustomed to getting her way, and I guess this time she decided that 'her way' would be to become better acquainted with me.

Now I'm certainly not prejudiced, but I'd just never been intimately or romantically involved with a white chic before. Janie and I did exchange conversation that was both engaging and enticing though, and something about her did spark my curiosity. I wouldn't say that I desired to approach her at the Underhill's party, but I'd be lying if I said that I failed to notice the firm round ass and firm breasts that occupied her petite and athletic frame. In addition to possessing physical characteristics similar to those of a sista', I was also intrigued by her opinions on music, art, and culture.

As if I didn't already have enough to stress over, I eventually agreed with Janie to "hang out sometime". Despite realizing the close relationship that Janie's family had with the Underhill's and also being fully aware of the potential ramifications, I convinced myself that I'd be able to juggle my relationship with Stacy, my job, a new fling with Janie, as well as the enormous assignment that I had to complete for Janie's father, Mr. Wilkens.

Operating within the confines of such close circles should've immediately set off sirens and red flags alerting me with a resounding "HELL NO" message. On the contrary though, I must have thought that I was as smooth as that daunting and flawless, womanizing player Marcus, depicted by Eddie Murphy in the movie *Boomerang*. For some reason, I honestly thought that I could pull it off without any hitches. Little did I know that embarking upon an intimate adventure with Janie would eventually aid in the suicide of my professional reputation and the sabotage of my career.

CHAPTER SIX
Doin' Too Much

Several weeks had passed, and the first day of July came on a dry and humid Thursday.

Like most days, my arrival home from work was both predictable and uneventful. The typical routine of parking in the garage, entering through the kitchen, and throwing my sport coat across the breakfast nook had become an all too familiar pattern. Moments later, I opened the refrigerator in desperate hope of stumbling across something tasty. To my dismay but not to my surprise, the contents were a far cry from being appealing. Three old boxes of pizza, a six-pack of Budweiser, and a head of wilted lettuce clearly spell out the word **B-A-C-H-E-L-O-R**. Deciding that the old pizza may not agree with my stomach, I opted for a much healthier meal of peanut M&M's and a cold beer. I headed out of the kitchen and into the den, where I laid on the couch and fished through the television channels, until finally deciding to settle for back and forth flipping between Sports Center and rap videos. Just as I became content and settled for a little evening relaxation, the phone rang with an unfamiliar number appearing on the caller-id screen. After three rings, curiosity finally got the best of me and I reluctantly answered the phone, disguising my voice as if I were asleep.

In a soft yawning voice, I softly uttered, "Hello."

The voice on the other line was that of a very overbearing and aggressive female, but I didn't recognize it immediately. My ploy of faking sleep was blatantly ignored as the piercing voice on the other line continued. Eventually, I recognized that this was the voice of Cathy Hightower. It had been two months since I'd stumbled across her at church, and I honestly wasn't expecting her to ever call. I knew that I certainly wasn't planning on calling her, so I guess I just assumed this to be a mutual feeling. As a matter of fact, I hadn't even kept up with her phone number.

As the conversation continued, I began to realize that it wasn't much of a conversation at all. She did most of the talking other than the few brief occasions in which I was given enough time to throw in an occasional "Okay", "Oh really", or a "Hmmmmm". Throughout the course of the phone call, I was reminded of all the reasons I'd never cared much for her to begin with. For some strange reason though, I agreed to see her in Kansas City the upcoming weekend. What the hell? It probably wouldn't be too bad. Plus, it wouldn't be a bad idea to leave town and take a break from Stacy for a weekend. The combination of working and sleeping with her had begun to take an overbearing toll on me.

So that Cathy didn't get the impression that I was anything less than a gentleman, I decided to feel her out by suggesting that I book a room for my weekend visit. Just as I expected though, she quickly offered her home.

"Now Cameron, you know I wouldn't make you drive two hours just to have you pay for a hotel. Boy, quit being silly; I'd be offended if you didn't stay with me. You can sleep in my guest room."

I insisted on getting a hotel room, but she continued pressing the issue that I stay with her. Reluctantly, I finally accepted her hospitable offer. For the next several minutes, she continued boring me with such an abundance of useless tidbits that I occasionally found myself nodding off. Of course, she became so engrossed in her own sensationalism that she never even noticed my blatant inattentiveness. Unable to tolerate another moment of her useless chatter, I finally requested the directions to her home, then I made and abrupt attempt to end the conversation.

My efforts were unsuccessful and she continued to drag on and on about how wonderful and smart she was, how envious everyone was of her, and of course - how much money she made.

Cathy was, and still is of those vain and arrogant types that make direct parallels between self-worth and net worth. She even foolishly equates intellect with collegiate credential. In other words, in her mind... anyone with a Masters degree is smarter than those with bachelors, and those with no degree at all are pretty much worthless pieces of shit. In her shallow way of thinking, anyone making a salary less than hers was equally worthless.

It would crush Cathy to know this, but she doesn't possess even a fraction of the intelligence of my ghetto princess Cheyenne. Not that this matters, but as far as income is concerned; Underhill has set up some investments for Stacy that have elevated her bankroll to a level that make Cathy's six-figure salary look like minimum wage. Nonetheless, even if no one else was convinced, Cathy had done a remarkable job of convincing herself that she was indeed a big shot.

I guess I should explain why she wanted me to visit in the first place. She was being recognized at her company's quarterly awards ceremony. For obvious reasons, I'm sure she found keeping a man's interest an extremely trying task. In fact, any sane man would avoid her all together. Obviously I'm not working with a full deck, since I continued to entertain her, despite the fact it's evident to me that she's overbearing, materialistic, unjustifiably vain and just plain unpleasant to be around. Let the record also state that although I did mention an improvement in her appearance since college, never once did I say that she was cute. She's just not ugly anymore! Furthermore, it's clear that the request of my presence is nothing more than her last minute act of despair to avoid attending Saturday's event without the company of a distinguished escort. Despite all this, I was actually anxious to attend. While vacationing in England last summer with Reggie, I had the good fortune of fitting for an Oswald Boateng suit. Prior to this time, I had been seeking an excuse to debut this fabulous garment. Saturday's function more than validated the opportunity to leave Cathy and her co-workers speechless.

Cathy and I continued to converse for a while, until our call finally ended with casual small talk about the upcoming weekend, and a simple 'Goodbye'. Upon ending the call with Cathy, I immediately contacted Stacy to inform her that I'd be leaving town for the weekend. Since she's already aware that I have relatives in Oklahoma City, I decided to tell her that I'd be there visiting cousins.

She seemed to buy it, and since she had already committed to attend a baby shower that weekend, I knew she wouldn't offer to tag along.

I figured the Oklahoma City excuse would cover me on Friday while with Cheyenne, and on Saturday while in Kansas City with Cathy. I was sure that Stacy would be calling all weekend, but I figured I could come up with an excuse for being inaccessible by cell phone later. More than likely, my lie would probably involve Reggie just as all my lies did. Besides, my philosophy on things of this nature had always been to deal with situations as they came, so I chose not to deal with the situation right then and there. I figured that I would be have ample time to deal with that drama later.

Speaking of drama and things to stress over, work was piling up daily and I still hadn't so much as even glanced at the Wilkens' files. Not to mention, several other deadlines were rapidly closing in as well. With that being said, this definitely wasn't an appropriate weekend to play the Casanova role, but I had already made commitments to be with Cheyenne on Friday and Cathy on Saturday. Besides, even if I were to stay home and be a good boy, I still probably wouldn't be too productive. I had become so uninspired that lately I had found myself just going through the motions rather than approaching work with the art and passion that had made me the rising star of Wallace, Underhill and Crabtree to begin with.

After listening to Cathy's annoying voice for nearly an hour, then dealing with Stacy's neuroticism for another half hour, I was too exhausted for words. I turned on the stereo and the soothing voice of Al Green's "Love and Happiness" was playing on the oldies station. I stretched out and relaxed; thinking about the irony of the words as my ears tuned in to every word of Al's trademark falsetto:

Love and happiness

Something that can make you do wrong
Make you do right
Love

With dress shoes, shirt, and slacks still on, I dozed off, ignoring the fact that I'd invested a small retirement plan into my wardrobe. One would've thought I'd take a little better care of my clothes, and usually I do. Some days though, life tends to make it difficult to really give a fuck! This was certainly one of those days.

CHAPTER SEVEN
Doin' Way Too Much

As sunlight crept through my living room window, I realized that Friday morning had come and I was still on the couch fully clothed. My face marinated in blinding spectrums of warm radiance, causing my eyes to squint and my forehead to wrinkle. I slowly rolled off the couch and onto my feet. Clumsily I stumbled towards the kitchen to glance at the digital clock on the microwave.

Suddenly startled, I snapped out of my morning reverie. Realizing that I had overslept, angry profanity escaped my lips and echoed throughout my empty home.

"Ohhhh fuck! I can't fuckin' believe I overslept!" - I screamed with both anger and disgust, appalled by my own irresponsible behavior.

It was 9:30 a.m. and I was scheduled to meet with Mr. Wilkens at 8:45 a.m. How on earth was I going to explain to Mr. Underhill that I'd missed an appointment with his most significant and prestigious client?

Operating under pressure, I grabbed the cordless phone and immediately called Underhill's office even before taking a second to think of what my lie would be. In the same motion, I ran towards the shower leaving a trail of clothes and shoes behind. I finally reached the bathroom, turned on the water, and checked its temperature with my hand. Finally, I positioned my naked body beneath the showerhead, just as the receptionist was answering the phone. Seconds later, I was transferred to Mr. Underhill's extension, and he answered – "Bill Underhill speaking."

He stated his greeting with extreme confidence and resolute authority, but I chose not to be intimated as I prepared to lie to my boss. I never called in sick, never arrived late, and I typically worked extra hours when required or requested. Therefore, I convinced myself that I would be let off the hook easy. I swallowed one time and began to speak, with the cordless phone crammed between my tilted neck and shoulder. Like mist that dissipates as morning makes way for the afternoon, milky soapsuds dissolved from my body while drops of warm water trickled gently down my chest and stomach.

Attempting to sound assertive, I firmly respond with, "Hey Mr. Underhill, this is Cameron."

Immediately interrupting me from uttering another word, Mr. Underhill angrily replied, "Where in the hell are you son, Wilkens has been waiting for you for damn near an hour!!!"

I knew that Underhill wasn't too big on excuses, but I also knew that although he's typically hard, he's never unfair. Plus, I had been hearing that he truly despised Stacy's former fiancé'

Logan. According to the guys working in the mailroom, Logan was pretty abusive towards Stacy, which is what finally led her back to Kansas. I had also heard from the mail guys that Logan was in town for the week, so I figured that Underhill had most likely caught wind of this too.

Still positioned beneath the running water, I prepared myself to deliver a lie that would go down in history as one of the smoothest exaggerated tales of all times. Without hesitation, I immediately allowed my voice to drop in volume and in a most sincere and expressive manner, I said: "Mr. Underhill, if I tell you something, you've got to promise me that you won't mention a word of this to Stacy. Please sir! I beg you, whatever you do… please don't say a word to Stacy regarding what I'm about to share with you."

Concern for his only child had overtaken Underhill, and his firm and authoritative tone suddenly shifted to reflect that of a concerned parent.

"What's wrong son… is everything okay with Stacy?" His voice trembled with anticipation and uneasiness as he spoke.

"Well sir, again… please don't tell Stacy this, but a couple of evenings ago, I dropped by Stacy's home to surprise her with roses. As I pulled up, I saw a strange character attempting to peep through her living room window. I yelled for the stranger to identify himself, but he ran off into the darkness. Sir... I tried to chase him down, but I didn't have much luck."

My voice had become intense, as the incredible lie continued to flow from my mouth. I knew that my last statement about being unable to catch Stacy's stalker really made my story sound believable. The mail guys had informed me that Logan was a track star while attending Stanford with Stacy. By now, Underhill had become livid as he interrupted me again. "What the hell is going on with Stacy son? Is everything alright?"

Though the shower water was beginning to turn cold, my story remained as fierce as hot lava, while I continued lying with flawless execution. Adding a sparse touch of anxiety to my already sincere and expressive tone, I replied, "Hold on sir, I-I'm going to tell you... I just...ewwww... pardon my French sir, but I'm just so fucking mad right now!" I paused and took two calculated deep breaths (one thousand one – one thousand two) then continued speaking into the telephone.

"I just really care about Stacy, and I'll be damn if I'm about to let a mother fucka' hurt her again. I'm sorry sir; please pardon my language. It's just that, I care so much about your daughter and it just pisses me off that some asshole thinks he can just..... UGGGHHHHHH!"

"Calm down son, everything is gonna be okay," - he advised me.

By then, the story was going so well that in a sick way, this act of deceit had become almost enjoyable. I continued to pile it on thick as I added more drama to my already spectacular tall tale. Underhill was already wrapped around my finger, but in the good spirit of not wanting to leave well enough alone, I transitioned my voice from a tone resembling anger to one resembling tears and pain.

"Okay sir, I'll calm down. Let's me just say this though."

I continued mumbling a series of frustrated words while maintaining an element of sadness in the temperament of my voice. I hadn't even mentioned Logan's name anywhere in the conversation. Nonetheless, I knew I had done a fabulous job of painting a picture that immediately pointed Underhill's finger in Logan's direction. Now it was time to go in for the kill and mention his name.

"I'd never met Logan sir. Hell, prior to today I couldn't have picked him out of a line-up. I just know that he's already put Stacy through enough bullshit, and I refuse to accept it. Maybe that wasn't even him at Stacy's window, but I heard that Logan was in town, and I know that his sole purpose for being here is to hurt Stacy. Then sir, I see some jerk stalking her home. My gut feeling was that it was Logan, and I just lost it. So this morning, as I was on my way to work, I got a call saying that Logan was hanging out at the barbershop on 13th Street. I know this is irresponsible on my part, but something just came over me and I immediately forgot all about work and headed to pay Logan a visit. Originally, I was going to simply ask him to step outside, so I could ask whether or not it was him I had seen outside of Stacy's and to inform him to stay away from her. Well this jackass attacked me. The fucker attacked me Mr. Underhill! I hope this doesn't make you think differently of me sir, but I was put in a situation. I had to defend myself Mr. Underhill. I had to sir, I didn't have a choice."

By now, my voice had become passionate and expressive, and I could see that I'd struck an emotional chord with Underhill. I assumed that the sound of the running shower water added a nice backdrop to the next line that I was about to deliver, so I turned the phone receiver directly towards the showerhead and spoke these words.

"Anyway Sir, I need to clean myself up and I'll be in shortly. I realize there's no excuse for being late and I'm willing to accept being held accountable. Regardless sir, I gotta protect Stacy and today I did what I had to do. I apologize."

After apologizing to Mr. Underhill for being late, our conversation had been overtaken by complete silence. Realizing that this was a situation where whoever speaks first loses, I waited him out until he finally took a deep breath, then began speaking, "Cameron... I thank God for you son. Stacy's intelligent, successful, and attractive, but when it has come to dating, she just can't seem to win for losing."

Then with a smile in his voice, he playfully asked, "Did you kick his ass son?"

With laughter in my voice, I replied with a humble "Yes" as if I were embarrassed about it. I could tell by Mr. Underhill's reaction that he was pleased with me defending his daughter's honor. Even if it was a bold faced lie, it nearly brought tears to Underhill to think that Stacy had found a companion who was just as passionate about her as he was himself.

Finally, Underhill offered to cover for me and reschedule my appointment with Wilkens for Monday morning. He and Wilkens had shared very solid business and personal relationships, so I'm certain that Wilkens was okay with whatever excuse Underhill provided on my behalf.

My phone call with Mr. Underhill ended, so I rinsed off and jumped out of the shower. Although it was 10:15 a.m. and I was extremely late for work, I still managed to complete every step of my morning hygiene ritual. I left the house at 10:50 a.m., and after stopping for a Krispy Kreme donut and a bottle of apple juice, I finally arrive at the office at 11:09 a.m. I spent the remainder of the day quite unproductively. Goofing around on the internet and replying to personal emails seemed to be the high priorities on my activities list. Occasionally Stacy would drop by my office just to say "hi" or to let me know that she was pleased with the direction our relationship was heading. She did ask once what my plans were for the weekend. As if I hadn't already lied enough for one day, I reminded her of the lie I had told her previously about going to Oklahoma City to visit family. Besides that though, five o'clock finally came and the day ended on a boring note, so I headed home to prepare for my evening with Cheyenne.

On the way home from work, I called Cheyenne to confirm that our date was still on for the evening. She seemed to be excited about it and requested that I pick her up at 9:00 p.m. We hadn't really planned out anything special, so I asked her what she'd like to do for the evening.

"It doesn't matter Cam, just as long as I get to spend it with you."

I made a few suggestions, including bowling and the movies. Neither activity seemed to entice Cheyenne, so she finally suggests that we rent movies and hang out at my crib. I knew that Stacy would probably be making random pop-ups to see if I was home, so that definitely wasn't a good idea. Therefore, I suggested that we get a hotel suite with a Jacuzzi tub. We maintained 9:00 p.m. as our rendezvous time and the conversation ended.

CHAPTER EIGHT
Check Out Time (WE GOTTA GO)

Something as simple as one rose
Or as childish as a love note
Sweet and sleepy like a lullaby
Wet and weepy like a teary eye
A destiny that can't be defined
By Kodak moments or Valentines
See what I'm feeling can't be defined
So I'm willing to give all that's mine
Just Listen

I had two small housekeeping items that needed tending to prior to my nine o'clock date with Cheyenne. First, I needed to touch base with Stacy to ensure that my Oklahoma City alibi was still copasetic. Then, I needed to reserve a hotel room for my evening rendezvous. On my way home from work, I made a call to The Kinsington Bed & Breakfast Suites. The Kinsington is on the outskirts of town, so I figured this to be a location that would minimize my risk of being spotted.

In order to avoid returning to the house, I decided to pack my things for K.C. in advance. This way, I could leave the hotel room the next morning and head towards K.C. immediately after checking out and taking Cheyenne home. Going back home would put me in jeopardy of Stacy possibly making a random check up and finding me there.

By the time I finished running errands, catering to Stacy, packing my bags, and reserving a room, it was damn near 7:00 p.m. I still had a couple hours to kill prior to picking up Cheyenne, so I left to purchase a variety of romantically alluring items. Then it was off to The Kinsington to get everything set up.

Being the hopeless romantic that I am, I decided to flatter Cheyenne with bold charm and subtle chivalry. Though the suites were already designed with romance in mind, I opted to heighten the ambiance with my own personal touch of flavor and pizzazz.

The suite itself was quaint, mysterious, and inviting. Though much smaller than your typical hotel suite, the room offered a sense of intimacy that more than compensates for what it lacked in size. Upon entering the room, a small hallway connected the approximate 20 feet that separated the front door from the bed. The quaint bathroom that sat off to the right of the hallway, for the most part was simple in design. The off-white ceramic tile floor and walls matched a similar off-white commode, pedestal sink and shower. Two complimentary robes hung from the hooks on the bathroom door. Also, a counter sitting off to the side of the sink housed a variety of neatly arranged items, including towels, shampoo, soap, and a small bottle of lotion.

The main attractions offered by the suite weren't visible until finally reaching the end of the hallway. A fabulous king sized bed was accentuated with oversized feather pillows, a heavily padded mattress, and four large wooden posts. The comforter hosted a multi-colored array of earth tones complimented by sparse droplets of majestic purple splendor. The creamy smooth textured, highly threaded linens are of the same beige complexion as the rich drapery covering the windows. Uniquely enough, the open area of the room contained a Jacuzzi hot tub which sat just a few feet to the left of the bed. Directly in front of the window and to the right of the bed, sat a cozy little table for two.

Rather than reaching into the bag of goodies I had purchased prior to arriving, I decided to dump its contents on the bed. A can of whipped cream, a carton of strawberries, assorted chocolates, a red light bulb, twenty-four candles, a bottle of bubble bath, baby oil, and a battery operated massage device occupied the bed. I had also purchased three dozen red roses that I had left in the car, so I hurried out and grabbed them along with a bottle of Remy Cognac, a pair of fancy drinking glasses, and a CD called "Perverted Excursions Volume I" by an artist named Mo B. Dick. Mo B. Dick had previously been a world-renowned rap producer, but was now enjoying huge success with a series of underground R&B releases designed specifically for setting sensual and erotic moods. I had a wild variety of intimate desires for Cheyenne; therefore, "Excursions" would provide an excellent soundtrack for the X-rated film I planned on directing and staring in.

Soon, it was 7:42 p.m. and I still needed to adorn the room and take a shower before picking up Cheyenne. Working with a sudden sense of urgency, I turned on the water to start filling the Jacuzzi and began strategically placing candles and roses throughout the room. Before long, a colorful blanket of passionate crimson surrounded the bed and the Jacuzzi. Also, every table, ledge, chair, and window seal was occupied with random arrangements of unlit vanilla candles and small plastic buckets filled with strawberries and chocolates. Water finally filled the tub, so I turned on the Jacuzzi jets and set the temperature at a comfortable 85 degrees. I added a cap full of warm vanilla sugar bubble bath, and what once was an ordinary tub had become a romantically alluring pool of vanilla scented foam. Six of the candles that I'd purchased were designed to float on water, so I gently placed each floating candle into the tub, being particularly careful not to wet the stems. I had five remaining roses, and by plucking the petals from each remaining stem, I created a scattered trail of springtime, which started at the front door and ended at the bed. The last few rose petals were sprinkled sparsely amid the Jacuzzi's active warm waters, blessing the bubbly potion with an appearance resembling red velvet raindrops.

On the nightstand between the tub and the bed, there sat a small CD player, a telephone, and a night light. I cued the Perverted Excursions album on the CD player and hid a three pack of Magnum brand condoms under the Gideon Bible in the pull out drawer. To make the mood more relaxing, I replaced the nightlight's white bulb with the red light that I'd purchased for the occasion. Since there was no refrigerator in the room, I requested extra ice buckets from the front desk, which I used to keep the Remy chilled, the whipped cream sweet, and the strawberries fresh. Finally, I placed the drinking glasses and the bucket containing the Remy on the ledge of the hot tub, lit all of the candles and stepped back to marvel my personal statement of erotic brilliance.

Like the ironic contrast sunlight burning the earth on a late winter evening, the red bulb and flickering candlelight combined to invoke similar dissonance, blending in unison and warming the room with passionate beams of cherry colored radiance.

At 8:17 p.m., my interior design work was complete. I needed to keep it moving if I planned on arriving promptly at

Cheyenne's, so I took a quick two minute glance over the room, then made mental notes of the how, what, and where activities I had planned for the night's occasion. An artificial plant and two room service menus occupied the quaint eating table, so I removed the items in case the two of us decided later to use the table as a canvas for displaying intimate expressions of artistic nakedness. In other words, I definitely planned on fucking this girl on the table.

At 8:22 p.m., I was finally in the shower, and by 8:50 p.m., I was comfortably dressed in blue jeans and a pink Polo shirt. I rushed out the door, jumped in the car, and drove well over the speed limit until finally arriving at Cheyenne's house at 10 minutes after nine. As I was about to knock on the door, Cheyenne's brother Jamal opens it up and offers me a seat in the living room. A few minutes later, Cheyenne entered the room wearing a stylish pair of sequined patterned jeans and a mid-drift t-shirt. Although she wasn't wearing any make-up this evening, Cheyenne was still stunning. Her high cheekbones accent a warm smile and full face, with thick hips and a round ass that nicely compliment her exceptionally large breasts. Her t-shirt was cut in a way that allowed just enough cleavage to tease the imagination, and her smooth textured skin contained the complexion of brown sugar blended with melted butterscotch candies. Her voluptuous titties were firm and perky, so it didn't matter that she wasn't wearing a bra. Besides, I figured she wouldn't be wearing much of anything once we got to the room, so this was one less item of clothing to remove.

At 9:26, Cheyenne and I arrived at the hotel, walked through the lobby, got on the elevator, and ultimately reached the room. Looking at the floor, Cheyenne noticed the one rose petal I had intentionally left on the outside of the door. She smiled and in a devilish tone asked;

"What are you up to Cameron?"

"Oh, nothing," I said, while slowly inserting the reader key into the slot and calmly pushing open the door. Holding her by the hand, I led her through the threshold and before we got to the bed, I pinned her against the wall in the narrow hallway. Immediately, she began massaging my head, shoulders, and the back of my neck - encouraging me to engage in kissing along her neck and shoulder, and gently nibbled on her ear. My left hand was firmly attached to her ass cheek, so she took hold of my right hand and deliberately directed it beneath her shirt. Soon, our mouths were connected and I became overtaken by an assortment of pleasant and erotic sensations as our moist warm tongues explored one another. She had eaten a box of hot cinnamon candies in the car, which enhanced the sweet flavor of her already delicious lips, while also enticing my taste buds with an alluring and numbing sensation.

Still passionately kissing one another and with hands still connected, Cheyenne guided my index finger and thumb around her firm right nipple. As my fingers began to manipulate; the throbbing of her rigid nipple and the shift in her breathing pattern united with a pleasant chorus of intimate moaning and careless whispers. Taking in a deep breath, in a choppy and almost crying murmur, she sighed; "Oh Cameron, I miss you so much. Baby why do you always make me wait so long?"

Immediately, I removed my hands from her ass and breast, and softly caressed her face with both hands. Passionately looking into her eyes, I continued to stroke the side of her face with my left hand as I allowed my right hand to slide across her face and mouth until only my index finger covered her lips.

"Shhhhhhhhhhhhhhhhhhhh" is all that was said, but such a gesture seemed to represent a thousand emotions. Immediately, she realized that too much talking would spoil the mood for me, so she inserted my index finger into her mouth and began fervently sucking. This deliberately stimulated my imagination and anticipation for oral pleasure.

With one hand gently stroking the side of her face and one finger in her mouth, I guided her through the hallway and towards the bed. An aquarium of exotic desires was there to greet her. Colonies of velvety textured rose petals swimming amidst crackling vanilla foam and warm flames of floating intimacy seemed to overwhelm her with delight.

Leading her past the Jacuzzi, I calmly laid her body sideways across the bed, allowing her feet to remain planted on the floor. Still clothed, I positioned my pelvic area between her legs and began a succession of thrusting and grinding movements. The two of us resumed the passionate kissing from earlier, but our mouths became much more active. Casual tongue tasting had been replaced by erotic outbursts of licking, biting, and sucking of lips. The intensity of our pelvic exchanges continued to increase, as I allowed my hands to slide inconspicuously beneath her t-shirt.

Eventually, I lifted her shirt just between the bottom of her chin and the top of her breasts. I moved my body over so that I lay on my side; facing Cheyenne, who was still resting on her back. This position granted me easier access to unclothe her, and I immediately began loosening her pants zipper with my left hand, while massaging her tasty nipple with my tongue. After several seconds of this maneuver, I finally had her belt unfastened and zipper undone. I continued allowing my active tongue to moisten her tender nipple, as my active imagination contemplated my next move. Finally, I built up the nerve to reach for more personal areas of her caramel coated body. As I continued to passionately suck and lick the areas between her breasts and upwards towards her neck and ears, I allowed my hand to slide slowly inside her cream colored lace panties. My fingers were now calmly caressing her warm, wet vagina and rapidly throbbing clitoris.

Delighted by my gesture, Cheyenne eagerly assisted my efforts and grabbed hold of her own panties with both hands. As she slid them off of her waist and around her voluptuous curves, I temporarily removed myself from being fluid and charming, and made an abrupt movement to position my body between her legs. With my head below her waist and the palms of my hands flat on the bed, I placed my teeth around her seductive lace undergarment. I began growling seductively on all fours in canine like fashion, as I tugged away at her panties with my teeth, until completely removing them from her body.

With her panties still dangling from my salivating mouth, I crawled towards her until we established eye contact. Still looking at her with intense passion in my eyes, I inserted my index and middle fingers into her moist crevice. The inner walls of Cheyenne's soft damp pussy contained the delightful texture of moist warm cotton. This utterly pleased my sense of feel, as the vibrant rhythm pounding between her thighs seemed to beat in perfect syncopation with her racing heartbeat.

Although the panties had fallen from my mouth, our eyes remain connected. With an intense look on my face, I licked my lips. Removing my fingers from her soaking wet vagina, I allowed my hand to glide upwards along the side of her body until finally embracing her face with my fingers. The flavor of her dripping womanhood still occupied my fingers. In a devilish fashion, I inserted my fingers into her mouth, allowing her to taste the sticky delicious sweetness of her own enticing fluids.

Tasting her own natural fluids seemed to increase her delight, as she became completely enthralled with sucking the delicious nectar from my moistened fingertips. Though eagerly anticipating the right moment to penetrate her inner walls, I contained myself long enough to progress to the next scene of tonight's sensual screenplay.

The candles shimmering in the darkness created the perfect backdrop for the next scene. I reached for the small plastic container of strawberries and the whipped cream I had purchased earlier. After placing both items beside me on the bed, I nibbled around Cheyenne's ankles until I had removed the socks from her feet. Then, with my tongue against her body, I crawled across her in animal like fashion. My mouth started at her ankle, moved along the side of her leg and hip, traveled inwards to her belly button, then up towards her t-shirt. I grabbed hold of her shirt with both hands and my teeth, and aggressively assisted her in escaping from her blouse.

Cheyenne, now sprawled across the bed, is completely naked with her legs spread apart. The faint sound of my cell phone ringing could be heard in the background, but the music from the stereo absorbed it and I continued to focus on Cheyenne. I got slightly nervous that it might be Stacy calling, but not so nervous that I allowed the blissful foreplay to end.

The augmented chemistry between us continued to progress rapidly. The mood enticed me to join Cheyenne in a shameless fellowship of unadulterated nakedness. I sat up on the side of the bed next to her and quickly removed each item of clothing from my body. Then I reached for the strawberries and whipped cream I placed on the bed earlier. I put one of the delicious red treats into my mouth and engaged in kissing her. Two moist tongues unite in matrimony to celebrate the strawberry's sweet sap, as our lips remained connected by the sinful fruit. Playfully, our tongues engaged in an explicit tug-o-war game, until I eventually loosen my lips in order to release the tasty scarlet aphrodisiac.

Cheyenne became temporarily pre-occupied with consuming the first strawberry, and didn't notice that I had reached for another. I placed the second strawberry into my mouth and repositioned my body until my head was between her soft warm thighs. Craftily utilizing my lips and tongue, I inserted the forbidden fruit into her creamy moist cleft until it was no longer visible. Like an abstract artist, I began spraying whipped cream around her naked canvas, while my tongue actively attempted to recover the lost strawberry. Finally, my taste buds connected with the delightful produce, and I curled my tongue back until the fruit was firmly fixated between my lips.

With the scrumptious strawberry again occupying my mouth, I allowed my tongue to eagerly consume the sugary vanilla foam surrounding her forest of succulent pleasures. Strawberry shortcake blended with buttery warm secretion, creating a soothing cool flavor, stimulating enchanting visions of promiscuous grandeur. Tradition may dictate that dessert be served after dinner, but I was working in reverse order. It was time for the main entrée, and I was no longer able to contain my desire for our bodies to become a commingled cloud of intimate lust.

I reached for the drawer where the condoms were strategically placed earlier, but she pulled me towards her until I could no longer reach them. I made another subtle attempt to move in the direction of the drawer, but again she pulled me towards her until our naked bodies were vertically positioned on top of one another.

At this point, the wise decision would've been to detach myself and make an abrupt move towards the drawer containing the condoms. Unfortunately, this didn't turn out to be the case. I obviously allowed the moment to dumbfound me, as her calming voice lured me away from any sense of rational thinking. In her most inviting voice, she whispered, "Cameron, I want you inside of me."

Despite knowing full well the risks associated with unprotected sex, the persuasive demeanor of Cheyenne Brown enticed me to make a stupid decision. The intensity continued to build, as I eagerly anticipated piercing the inner realm of her delightful flesh corridor. With a moist stream of passionate femininity awaiting me, I had become so rigid that my throbbing erection was as discomforting as it was provocative. I couldn't wait another second, and before long my bare, erect limb was consumed by her tender soft tissue. Tightly connected bodies began flowing in and out of one another in harmonious unison like the fluidity of ocean waters. We engaged in assorted symphonies of vertical and horizontal fantasies as glowing candles continued to burn and the music played softly in the background.

Continuing to make love to her, I rested my head on one of her large round morsels and attached my mouth to the other. My tongue moved across and around the firm sweet nipple while my lips were sucking the surrounding area. After several moments of this display, I eventually detached my mouth from her voluptuous pacifier and lifted my head. Planting my palms on the bed, I lifted my body semi-vertically above her and glanced down to catch a glimpse of my own inward and outward strokes. Using both hands, she grabbed hold of herself, and quickly inserted her own right nipple between her full round lips. I placed my mouth on the same nipple, and our tongues playfully fondled one another as we shared in the tasting of her delectable chocolate mound.

Over the course of the next 90 minutes, we continued to engage in endless episodes of passionate affection. She seemed more than satisfied, as overtures of clitoral orgasms provided intricate preludes for an ensemble of melodic vaginal opuses. A mixture of sour teardrops and sweet tasting sweat set the stage for a dramatic contrast, resembling the popular theater masks representing comedy and tragedy. The finale was just moments away; Cheyenne planted her soft sweaty palms against my chest, and aggressively thrust against me until our positioning reciprocated that of our previous pose. With me now lying flat and Cheyenne in control, she moved her head below my waist and began swirling her damp tongue along the tip of my sensitive rigid band. I was incapable of containing myself any longer so I reached for the back of her neck and pulled her towards me until her mouth completely absorbed my severely swollen swipe. My body weakened as my fists clinched and toes curled. Within a matter of seconds, warm liquid zeal escaped my frozen torso, oozing effortlessly as she fervently devoured the freely flowing masculine liquid.

She got up from the bed and headed to the bathroom, and I heard my phone ringing in the background again. I was certain it was Stacy calling, but at this point, I wasn't even concerned. However infrequently they may have been, I did enjoy the moments that Cheyenne and I spent together; therefore, I hoped not to let my nervous anxiety ruin the evening.

She returned to the room, reached for her purse and pulled out a stick of marijuana, pre-rolled in a gutted cigar wrap. Then she walked to the Jacuzzi in the middle of the room and reached in with her hand to check the temperature of the water. Soon after, she blew out the flames from the floating candles, poured in another cap full of bubble bath, turned the jets back; then concealed her naked body beneath refreshed bubbles and soggy rose petals. On the ledge of the tub, the cognac was still chilling on ice, so she poured two glasses, lit her home rolled smolder, and invited me to join her in the tub. As we soaked together in the soothing waters, enjoying our cognac, I realized how wonderful it felt to have her near me.

Again, the sound of my phone rang in the background. Though the music no longer played, the Jacuzzi motor still somewhat absorbed the annoying ring tone. I sat next to Cheyenne and admired her as she inhaled and exhaled the cloudy potion, and I realized just how much she meant to me. I'm not sure if she felt the same, but I became frustrated that society had dictated rules that made it impossible for us to truly be together. She'd become victim to a rule that made her feel worthy of only thugs and drug dealers. I, on the other hand, had become so whitewashed in bureaucracy that I'd lost sight of my own identity. Rather than following my heart, I continued to be stuck with boring, high-post, spoiled little rich girls - like Stacy. If only I could've learned to follow my heart rather than chasing after a perception that society had established for me. I often ask myself what songs I would have on the soundtrack to my life. I'm not sure how the complete album would sound, but I am certain about one thing -- the voice that best described Cheyenne and I would be Erykah Badu, somberly and soulfully crying "I guess I'll see you next lifetime".

After we finished our drinks and Cheyenne was through smoking, we climbed out of the tub, and crawled into the bed; allowing the covers to dry our naked wet bodies. Holding her in my arms, we fell fast asleep and remained asleep throughout the night.

The next morning, I was awakened by nervous taps on the shoulder, as Cheyenne seemed panicky and uneasy. I was uncertain as to why she seemed so troubled, but I assumed it had something to do with K-9. Perhaps she worried that he knew she hadn't been home. Maybe she wanted to get there before he started calling or driving by. Who knew? Maybe she was afraid that he might see me taking her home. The original plan was for me to have her home by 8:00 a.m., and to be on the highway by 8:45 a.m. headed to Kansas City, but I guess we both overslept.

As she continued tapping me on the shoulder, I finally regained consciousness, rolled onto my back, and stretched my body from head to toe. I stared aimlessly at the ceiling and took a moment to briefly ponder the wonderful evening the two of us had just shared. It appeared as if she had already gathered our things and taken a shower, and she anxiously waited for me to do the same. As I attempted to roll over and resume sleeping, she aggressively shook me, and in a nervous voice yelled out, "Cameron, its eleven o'clock... Check out time. We gotta go"

I took a quick shower, put on my clothes and we left the hotel en route to Cheyenne's house.

As we lay here looking at the ceiling –
Both enjoying the feeling
I love the way we lay here –
But you know that we can't stay here
As we enjoy the pleasure – We must take the measures
To keep this on the cool
Don't catch no attitude
It's time to go

CHAPTER NINE
Another Day in the Life of…

It's still Saturday and I'm within seconds of approaching Cheyenne's street. As we turn the final corner and approached the house, she seemed to be relieved that there were no signs of K-9. As I pulled next to the curb, she kissed my cheek and thanked me for the previous night. I smiled and suggested that we see one another again soon. She opened the car door to leave, and just as she did, a jet black Mercedes came barreling around the corner in a reckless fashion. Of course it was none other than K-9. I suppose he'd driven by several times throughout the night and this morning, and now he'd seen enough to make him livid. The out of control vehicle rapidly approached, and I could see that Cheyenne was afraid. By this time, I was just flat pissed off.

"What the fuck is wrong with this stupid ass nigga?" I angrily asked her.

She just cringed, shrugged her shoulders, and with tears rolling along the side of her face, made a desperate request for me to leave.

"Cameron, just leave… Please don't say nothing to him babe… just leave."

Cheyenne jumped out of the car and raced towards the house as K-9 drove up the driveway, into the grass, and in front of the porch. As she made an attempt to open the front door, he rushed towards her and snatched away her keys. I briefly pondered the idea of getting out and assisting her, but I knew she'd prefer that I stay out of it, so I abided by her wishes. Besides, I doubted anything other than the typical shoving, yelling, and arguing would take place. The two of them continued to engage in cursing and name calling, as I drove away and wondered what would become of the conflict. Before long, I was on the highway and no longer giving the situation much thought.

During my drive, I checked my voicemail. Although there were three messages from Stacy, I was surprised to see that none of them were angry or confrontational. In fact, they were actually rather pleasant.

She wished me a safe trip to Oklahoma, encouraged me to have a nice time with my cousins, and let me know that I was missed. In order to make myself look good, I called her from the highway and pretended to be in Oklahoma City. She inquired about my cousins, so I pretended to be lost after running errands, and convinced her that I was driving around Oklahoma City looking for their house.

"I really miss you," she said playfully after a few minutes of meaningless chitchat.

"I miss you too baby. How are you?'

"I'm okay. Are you having fun with your cousins?"

"It's okay. I haven't really done much other than sleep so far. I was kinda tired when I got here last night. And now, my ass is lost... go figure!"

"I see" she said laughing. "I know my baby needs his rest. Especially so you can be ready for momma when you get back in town. You need me to let you go so you can call and get directions?"

"No babe, I'm good. If I don't see something familiar in the next few minutes, I'll get off the phone. I think I can find it though."

She went on to express how eager she was to seduce me when I returned on Monday. Although she wouldn't be missed at all during my weekend vacation from her, I somehow mustered up the energy to proclaim to her my love. I said, "I love you, I miss you, and I can't wait to see you Sunday."

As if that wasn't bad enough, I somehow ended up suggesting that she go to Frederick's of Hollywood and purchase something sexy for Camillia to wear on Sunday.

Oh yeah, I guess I should explain who Camillia is before I go any further.

Stacy and I role-played sometimes, and Camillia is one of the characters we created. I know we sound like a couple of weirdo's, but it was actually pretty fun once we got into it. Besides, she really got on my fucking nerves, so I needed something extra to make our situation at least somewhat interesting.

The scene starts out with me pretending to be Columbus Pickens; a multi-millionaire oil tycoon from Texas. I would go into a heavy Texas accent, wearing the boots, the hat, the whole nine. In our twisted role-play, my family employed Camillia as the housemaid. We usually dressed her in the seductive maid outfits that the lingerie shops sell, and she walked around with a feather duster, bending over to dust off the furniture while deliberately propping her ass in the air, or seductively adjusting her bustier. Stacy used an accent when playing Camillia as well. It wasn't a very good accent, so the attempted South American dialect often sounded like a poor island imitation. Nonetheless, it still turned me on from the standpoint that I really got into pretending it to be someone other than Stacy.

To make a long story short, the scene always ended with the two of us sneaking into the guest-house while my wife and kids were asleep in the main quarters. It's too funny; we actually went through the whole motion of being discreet and even getting quiet when we pretended to hear noises of people approaching.

For several minutes, we laughed together as we continued making date arrangements for Columbus and Camillia. Finally, still pretending to be lost, I ended our conversation and continued my drive. A couple of hours passed, and before I knew it, I was pulling into Cathy Hightower's Driveway in Kansas City, Missouri. It was 3:00 p.m.

CHAPTER TEN
Bitch Please !!!

I won't go into great detail about Cathy's home, or any of the boring ass conversations that she and I had during the afternoon. I'll just say that her home was nice and very well decorated. After helping me get my things situated in the guest room, she offered to take me to lunch. The awards dinner didn't start until 8:30 p.m., so we had a few hours to kill prior to then. We ended up eating wings at a local sports bar; then hanging out at the mall for a while. Of course, Cathy did most of the talking throughout the day, so I pretended to listen attentively while Cathy bragged on and on about how wonderful and fabulous a person she was. I immediately started questioning myself for even making this trip as she continued to ramble aimlessly. When we arrived back at her home, it was seven o'clock, so she suggested that we start getting dressed. She got me a bar of soap and some clean towels and directed me towards the guest bathroom.

Then she headed toward her room to prepare herself for the night's occasion.

I'd been to a few corporate awards functions, so I had an idea of what to expect. Typically, a vice-president flies in town to conduct the ceremony. Ladies are draped in fabulous gowns, and gentlemen sport black-tie and elegant dinner coats. Like most competitive environments, I knew Cathy and her peers probably weren't too fond of each another. Still, I made the correct assumption that she and her co-workers would remain in one another's space for most of the evening, wearing fake smiles and pretending to enjoy one another's company. Then, once the lights faded and the music no longer played, they would all go home and talk about each other like dogs. Welcome to Corporate America! Of course, Cathy wanted nothing more than to be viewed as a big-shot, so I figured she blended into this sick matrix quite well.

I showered and got dressed. As I mentioned before, I wore a tailor made Boateng design. Oswald Boateng designs for many of today's music, entertainment, and sports stars. In fact, he provided some of the wardrobe for Jude Law in the movie *Alfie*. Honestly speaking, there was nothing flashy about my attire in the way of color or patterns. That wasn't the intent of this particular garment. What did separate this suit from your typical after-five wear is that it draped my shoulders, chest, and waist perfectly. So perfectly, that one quick glance revealed that without question, this outfit was crafted specifically for Cameron Banks. Who would've thought that a million dollar smile, a two-carat diamond earring, and an expensive blend of European fabric could make a black and white ensemble look so colorful. I glanced in the mirror while adjusting my bowtie and pocket silk and immediately imagined myself on a rat-pack poster, joyously celebrating with Dean Martin and Frank Sinatra on my left and right sides. Continuing to daydream in the mirror and still in awe of my own elegance, I smiled... pretended to be holding a martini, and in my best English dialect, I recited the words "Bond... James Bond."

For a few more minutes, I continued entertaining myself in the mirror, and then migrated to the living room. To my surprise, Cathy was there waiting and ready to go.

"You look adorable Cameron-" she said, with a smile on her face.

I returned the compliment. "You look great too Cathy."

To be completely honest, my politically correct compliment was quite the exaggeration. Although she didn't look bad, she definitely didn't look ravishing enough to be on my arm for the evening, or even in the same room as me for that matter. Now I'm not saying that she looked like a prostitute, but I felt like Richard Gere next to Julia Roberts in "Pretty Woman". We just didn't look like we belonged together.

I could go into precise artistic detail in describing her attire, but it won't be necessary. Her cosmetic jewelry, heavily applied make-up, and pedestrian dress could best be illustrated with one simple word – BORING! Immediately, I realized that agreeing to attend was definitely a bad idea, but I decided to make the most of it and we departed for the banquet.

As I had anticipated, the banquet was lavish and elegant.

Though a little pink, my filet mignon was superb. During the cocktail hour, a string quartet serenaded spectators sipping champagne from crystal glasses as company execs wearing reluctant facial expressions, mingled with front line sales persons and first tier managers. These type of functions usually humored me since there's always at least one person in attendance who tries way too hard to demonstrate class. That night, I was stuck escorting that individual, so that time it didn't amuse me. In fact, it embarrassed me.

Then there's always one other person who just doesn't get it. It took about five seconds to spot this character, even before entering the building. As the valet took Cathy's car keys, and we started our stroll along the red carpet, the next car pulling up was a stretch limo. Unable to contain my curiosity, I glanced over my shoulder and saw a brother getting out of the car wearing a navy colored suit straight from the Kings of Comedy collection. To top it off, dude had on a matching navy hat, a pair of navy gators, and navy tinted shades with a playboy bunny logo in the bottom corner of the left lens. I can't remember the brother's real name, but all of his co-workers kept calling him "Slick". All bullshit aside, this was truly one funny ass nigga, but he must've been damn good at selling software. By the end of the evening, ole' Slick had cleaned up on the awards.

After dinner and the formal awards presentations, the string ensemble was replaced by a disc jockey playing popular tunes. For some reason, I wasn't surprised that Sir-Mix-a-Lot's 1992 Smash "Baby Got Back" was the track chosen to get the party kicked off. Rhythm-less white people, corny acting brothers, and a mixture of everyone else quickly crowded the dance floor. Of course, my man Slick quickly became the center of attention. As the music continued, Slick joyously led the crowd in the Electric Slide, the Macarena, and even the Cotton

Eyed Joe. I know this is dead wrong, but while The Macarena was playing, and the more Slick danced, the more "Hey Macarena" started to sound like "Hey It's A Nigga". By the end of the song, I was pointing a finger at Slick and laughing, while singing my version along with the popular melody.

"That's a nigga, you're a nigga, he is a nigga... Hey Slick's A Nigga!"

Of course, Cathy - the self-proclaimed queen of sophistication wasn't amused, because she was too busy flaunting me around like a show-n-tell exhibit. I guess she needed me to get back on my best behavior again, since she was desperate in her attempt to make a good impression.

We mingled with several of her peers for the remainder of the evening, as she deliberately attempted to flaunt her very limited and often incorrect understanding of everything from finance and money, to politics, government, and religion. Though several questions were asked of me throughout the evening, Cathy took the liberty of answering most of these for me. She even took the liberty of answering almost every question she'd asked in the first place. Never had I witnessed someone make such an ass of themselves in such a pitiful attempt to look important.

Cathy and I eventually found ourselves standing on the outside terrace, amidst the company of several of the attendees that night. Among the individuals in our presence were two well groomed, middle aged white men and a fairly attractive Asian lady who looked to be about 40 or so. I discovered that they were a regional vice president, an executive level director, and a regional director of Cathy's firm. I decided that I wouldn't let Cathy continue embarrassing me with her idiot responses. I intercepted her before she was able to ignite another painful conversation.

I extended my hand, smiled, and introduced myself while stepping in front of Cathy as we approach the trio of executives.

"Hello, I'm Cameron Banks - How's everyone this evening?"

Cordial head gestures accompanied handshakes and smiles as I commanded their attention. Employing basic psychology, I charmed the executives by simply putting them on a pedestal. I started by first complimenting the lady and then complimenting the event.

"Ma'am, I must say that you look and smell wonderful this evening. What is that fragrance? Is that Caron Nuit de Noël?"

The Asian executive was immediately surprised and impressed by my knowledge of the French perfume. She smiled devilishly and then she asked, "What do you know about Nuit de Noel, Mr. Banks?"

Rather than informing her that this was one of my mother's favorite fragrances, or running down the complete history of the perfume and boring her to death, I kept it simple and stated, "Well ma'am, they say that the scent was designed to capture the festive spirit of Christmas Eve. If this is indeed true, then I must say that you do wear it well."

As she and I mutually engaged in a laugh, the two middle-aged gentlemen joined the conversation, and the three of us embarked upon discussing a gambit of business, social, and political items.

Cathy attempted to blend in, but her limited knowledge of current events hindered her. Before long, she was nodding her head, smiling, agreeing, and pretending to be knowledgeable of the topics being discussed. Her blatant insecurities wouldn't allow her to bear the thought of being less informed than me, so I could see why she tried to convince me of her make believe social prowess. I could even see why she tried to convince her co-workers and company execs. What's sad though is that more than anything, she appeared to be trying to convince herself. What a fucking idiot!

After mingling a while longer, we decided to leave early and head back to her place. We arrived back at her house by midnight. I had planned on sleeping in the guest room – so, as we entered the front door, I yawned and said - "Arrrrhhhhhhhh....

I'm so tired. If you don't mind, I think I'll head on into the guest room to crash."

Of course, she wasn't having any of that. As annoying as she was, I'm sure it didn't take long for her to run off any man that half way showed an interest, so I guess she wasn't ready to relieve me of her company.

"Cameron, you're sleepy already? I wanted you to have a cup of coffee with me."

Reluctantly, I agreed to join her for a cup of coffee after I hung up my suit and changed into a t-shirt and a pair of basketball shorts.

When I returned, she had changed also, now wearing a pair of sweats and a sports bra.

As we engaged in conversation and coffee drinking, I found myself struggling to stay awake. Occasionally, I yawned and batted my eyes in an attempt to avoid being rude and falling asleep. Just when I was unable to bear another moment of useless banter, she mentioned that she was about to take a shower. I was about to be off the hook. I silently celebrated, as the opportunity to go to bed and no longer hear her irritating voice presented itself. Then, I was suddenly put in a trick bag when the next question escaped her mouth.

"Cameron, you wanna take a shower with me?"

I'm not the least bit attracted to Cathy, because she's annoying as hell. Every thought, idea and voice inside of me was loudly yelling "HELL NO BITCH!" Nonetheless, I smiled, disposed of my shirt, chuckled, and with an heir of confidence I replied, "Sure I'll take a shower with you."

Minutes later, we were in the master bedroom shower butt ass naked. The sight of Cathy's aging naked body was a sight less than impressive, and I became disgusted with myself for allowing myself to become involved in this situation. It was too late to turn back now though, so I pretended that her sagging breasts and bowling pen shaped body didn't exist. As she moved towards me, I tried to imagine the faces of various other lovers in a demented attempt to escape the thought of the undesired intimacy that was just moments away. She wrapped one arm around my neck, while kissing and biting on my chest. Her other hand was massaging my shoulder and side with a bar of soap. Again using my imagination, I squinted my eyes just enough to see the image of a woman but not enough to clearly focus on the particular image of Cathy. She continued biting on my naked body, moving from my chest to my stomach and waist. By the time she finally fell to her knees to engage in providing oral pleasure, I began to imagine everyone from Stacy and Cheyenne, to celebrities like Halle and Janet. I soon discovered that even my warped imagination and partially squinted eyes couldn't remove me from this less than desirable position, so I opened my eyes and faced the bitter reality that we were about to have sex. I was eager to get this over with, so I lifted her by the chin until she was upright on her feet. After turning the water off, we then escorted one another to her contemporary styled, queen sized bed. Unable to muster the energy to be passionate, artful, or imaginative, I made this moment as simple and plain as possible. I picked her up, placed her frail wet body on the bed, grabbed a condom that I had stashed in my sock and assumed a missionary position with my face buried in the pillows. Slowly, I began thrusting in and out of her oddly shaped body while my mind was occupied with irrelevant items like the tax code, the United States Constitution, and Rudy Ray Moore movies. To say the least, I was bored to death. Her pitiful attempts to talk dirty didn't help matters much. The sound of her voice was as noxious as thoughts of desert vultures gnawing on decayed rodents. After 30 minutes or so, the less than stellar intercourse session had concluded and I pretended to immediately fall asleep. She then made several attempts to spark conversation and to cuddle against me, but I continued to fake sleep, hoping to avoid the discomfort that accompanied conversing with her.

Eventually, I fell into a deep sleep and didn't regain consciousness until 9:30 a.m. Sunday morning. Awakened by the smell of freshly brewed coffee, sweet Danish pastries, fruits, and turkey bacon, I realized that my chances of immediately getting the hell out of Cathy's house had gotten slim.

Instinctively, I opened my eyes, stretched, and rolled in the direction of the enticing aroma. I turned to find her waiting to deliver breakfast in bed from a fancily decorated serving tray.

"Hey baby, I made you breakfast. Come on and wash up so we can eat."

Reluctantly, I crawled out of the bed and made my way to the sink. While brushing my teeth, she spoke again, this time with a combination of excitement and playful laughter in her voice.

"Baby... If you hurry up, we might have time to do it again before church."

All I could think of was, "WOW! She wants to fuck me and then take me and show me off at church." I didn't plan on getting intimate with Cathy again, nor did I plan on attending church. Unfortunately for me though, her aggressive type-A personality took over and I couldn't think fast enough to make up a reasonable excuse. To make a long story short, we engaged in another lackluster sex session, showered, got dressed and attended church together. Ironically enough, I hadn't even realized that it was the 4th of July until I saw the date printed on the church bulletins. July 4th sex with Cathy was about as disappointing as the 4th would be for the only kid on the block without fireworks.

After church, nothing particularly exciting happened. I went back to Cathy's house where she continued to annoy me. I then eventually gathered my things, changed clothes, and at around three in the afternoon, I got on the highway and headed back home. Disgusted with myself, I pondered as to why I even made this trip in the first place, what Cathy's expectations would be going forward, and what lies to tell Stacy. Oh well… I guess the songwriter was right. "Life goes on – long after the thrill of living is gone!"

CHAPTER ELEVEN
Monday Mornings

The date was Monday, July 26^{th,} and the first thing on my agenda was to get busy on my work for Mr. Wilkens. Up to this point, I had really dropped the ball on the Wilkens project, so I was going to have to work my ass off to get back on pace. As I mentioned previously, Wilkens is one of the wealthier and more powerful men in Kansas and is a very valued client of our firm. In other words, screwing this up would definitely cost me my job. This particular project involved Wilkens' plans to buy out two other companies, and my job was to compile a list of financial statements, reports, and feasibility charts to illustrate whether or not this merger would make profitable business sense. I was scheduled to make a report to Wilkens and his board of directors in three weeks, and I had about six weeks worth of work to do, so it was imperative that I got focused. I arrived at the office at 7:15 a.m., and though I'd had the Wilkens' files for well over two weeks, I was just getting around to sorting through the multiple stacks of paperwork. By 8:10 a.m., I realized that some of the information I needed was missing, so I made a call to Wilkens and informed him of the additional documents that I needed. Wilkens sounded slightly concerned that I was just now requesting these documents, but he didn't dwell on it for too long. "Cameron!! How about if I just send all the files home with Janie, and you can swing by and pick them up later this morning," he suggested, since his house was close to the office."

    I agreed to this, and by ten o'clock, I was standing on the lawn of the Wilkens' estate. Though the home was indeed gorgeous, it wasn't exactly what I expected. I guess I had anticipated seeing some interesting landscaping or something of character that made a statement about the owner. I suppose a million dollar home makes a statement in itself, so perhaps the other frills aren't necessary.

    I walked up the driveway, past Janie's convertible Porsche, up the stairs, and rang the doorbell. Janie greeted me at the door wearing a tight pair of pink hip hugging shorts and a white tank top.

Other than Janie's surprise call earlier this month, the only other time that I'd met her was at the Underhill dinner party, so I didn't expect much of a conversation exchange. I figured, she'd hand me a box of files and send me on my way. To my surprise though, things transpired much differently.

"Come in and have a seat, Cameron."

I took a seat in the living room and marveled at her wonderful life. Here it is 10:00 a.m., and she was lounging around the house watching soaps.

Wilkens had originally sent Janie off to school at his alma mater, Duke University. After a semester, she decided to drop out and attend art school in Denver, Colorado. Of course, she didn't stay interested in art too long either, and after experimenting with a culinary academy, community theater, and managing a rock band, she finally decided to take a vacation from 'finding her-self'.

She took a seat beside me. She was a fairly attractive white girl, but other than friendship, involvement with her was the furthest thing from my mind. Mistakenly, I thought this was the furthest thing from her mind as well. That is, until she began asking questions.

"So Cameron, I didn't get much of a chance to talk to you at the dinner party. Tell me about yourself. What do you like doing in your spare time?"

I answered a few questions about my life and my favorite past times, then we somehow got on the subject of Stacy.

"So I hear that you and Stacy are quite the item!"

By then, I was getting rather sick of everyone making the assumption that I was just madly in love with Stacy, so I corrected her right away.

"I respect Stacy, but everything isn't always what it seems, Janie."

She continued to pry for information to the point of almost being bothersome; then she made a statement that blew my mind.

"So... Cameron! Have you ever been involved with a white girl?"

Actually, I hadn't been and I really didn't have much aspiration of doing so. Something about her straightforward assertiveness made me consider otherwise though. Realizing that trouble was right around the corner, I decided to engage in this conversation anyway."

"No, I can't say that I have. Why would you ask me that?" I said in a rather flirtatious manner.

Smiling and moving closer to me on the living room sofa, she touched the side of my face and looked deeply into my eyes.

"Oh, no reason." She said with a smile on her face. "To tell you the truth, I just find you attractive, and if you say that it's not that serious between you and Stacy, then I trust you that it isn't."

She laughed and with an evil tone said, "Besides, I wouldn't care if it were serious. I'm not trying to marry you, I just find you interesting. Plus, we've known the Underhill's forever, and I've never cared much for that bitch Stacy in the first place."

She paused momentarily, before unleashing an outburst of evil laughter. Then in an equally mischievous tone, continued speaking.

"I wanted to talk to you at the Underhill party, but Stacy and her parents never seemed to give you room to breath."

Her fingers continued stroking my face, and by this time, our eye contact had become intimate and suggestive. Suddenly enticed by the dream-like haziness of her fervent eyes, I leaned in her direction until our lips connected. In a somewhat aggressive manner, her tongue penetrated my lips, and soon our tongues engaged in a passionate and suggestive exchange.

A minute or so passed, and her hand slowly slid down my chest and stomach, to my waist. Before long, she had loosened my belt and zipper and began a series of rhythmic hand massaging motions along the areas below my waistline. Out of respect for my job, I tried to pull away from her and get things back on a business pace, but she aggressively lunged forward as I attempted to pull myself apart.

Soon, I was lying on the couch with her lying on top of me, kissing my mouth and neck, and busily loosening my tie and unbuttoning my shirt. I'm not sure what type of perfume Janie was wearing, but her body possessed the sweet and delightful aroma of warm vanilla and tasty cinnamon.

At this point, my carnal desires seemed to overshadow any longing to demonstrate nobility and moral turpitude, and though I was wise enough to know better than continuing on with this precarious display of affection, my raging temperature for passion and lust seemed to overtake me.

Janie seemed equally excited, as she allowed her body to roll off mine, taking hold of my hand and leading me up the stairs, down a long hallway, and finally into her parents' room.

I've been in some expensive homes before and have even witnessed some amazing bedroom designs, but I can honestly say that I'd never seen a bedroom quite like this amazing master suite. The Victorian style divan was the size of nearly two king sized beds, and its majestic frame sat so high that step stools occupied both sides in order to allow comfortable access to the full feathered mattresses. Approximately six feet from the bed was a walkout balcony that overlooked the estate's natural bodies of water and wooded terrain. The fireplace at the foot of the bed was built into the wall separating the master bathroom from the main area of the bedroom, allowing the fireplace to be enjoyed from either room. The face of the fireplace was white Italian marble, with matching white marble surrounding its base. The same marble tile occupied the walls and floor of the bathroom, which also featured a shower the size of a small bedroom, a magnificent Jacuzzi tub, and a small plasma television directly across from the commode.

    I won't go into great detail about my Monday morning rendezvous with Janie, but I will say this, whoever it was that coined the myth that white men can't jump, obviously didn't watch much basketball, and if anyone has ever said that white women don't have rhythm, they obviously had never met Janie. By the time the morning was over, I was pretty certain that Janie's body had touched every single wall of her father's massive bedroom. Afterwards, I went to the closet and dug out a pair of pajamas and a robe, and immediately went into playing the role of Wilkens. As if Janie wasn't already amused, her laughter grew to hysterical proportions when I began mimicking her father's raspy and deliberate voice, lecturing her on all of the reasons why she shouldn't date black men. What was probably even funnier to her was that I bet she'd actually heard very similar lectures from her old man on many occasions.

We continued to engage in useless recreation for a few minutes, and then I gathered my things. As I was pulling up my slacks and fastening my belt, Janie asked me the oddest question.

"Penny for your thoughts Cameron... Was it as good for you as it was for me?"

As I had mentioned previously, I hadn't spent much time with white women, and already, I had realized that the 'no rhythm' rumor wasn't true. I guess I also discovered that they aren't too bashful around black men either. Honestly speaking, the sex was spectacular, but I didn't want her to get too bigheaded, so I pondered for a while, pretending to be giving the question some thought. I then took a slow deep breath and nonchalantly answered Janie's bold question with a slight smirk on my face.

"It was cool."

Then, in a silly and childish manner, I let out a playful laugh, and continued speaking.

"Actually Janie, it was real cool."

Janie smiled, and in the spirit of mischievous youth, she engaged in another question.

"So, what are you doing next Monday around this same time?"

Without much arm-twisting, I eagerly agreed to meet Janie for a rendezvous the following Monday, which led to an additional rendezvous the Monday morning after that. Before long, Monday mornings had become a tradition with she and I... a tradition the two of us began to jokingly refer to for several Mondays to come, as 'The Monday Special'

CHAPTER TWELVE
Finally a good day

On Friday, August 6th, I didn't have anything special planned. Stacy had been bugging me about going to a hair show that one of the local magazines sponsored every year. The publication was called "CONTEMPO MAGAZINE", and the publishers did a great job of incorporating local style and culture into the hair and fashion magazine. Typically, close to 800 guests attended this event each year. I've attended this function in the past, but this time I chose not to go, since I knew that Stacy and Cathy would both be attending.

Cathy typically doesn't miss opportunities to come to town and be seen, and this event was one of the 'who's who' gala of galas that would provide her an opportunity to perpetrate the big shot role that she's so accustomed to portraying. She had called me a few times during the week to inform me that she'd be in town, so I knew for sure that she'd be bugging me to make time for her.

In case I haven't stated it enough, Cathy is not attractive, not likeable, and boring in bed. But, for some reason, I continued to entertain her. For the life of me, I still can't explain why - even to this day. Of course, I reluctantly agreed to see Cathy later on Friday night, following the hair show.

Many of my friends have often jokingly referred to me as a man of multiple personalities. Reggie has even gone as far as saying that if I were involved with two separate women who didn't know one another, and their paths just so happened to cross; if they were to engage in a conversation where each of them described this 'fabulous guy' they were fortunate enough to be involved with, they could potentially leave that conversation thinking that they were discussing two completely different dudes; especially if my name weren't to come up in the conversation.

As fate would have it, this strange and unlikely circumstance took place on the night of the hair show. I wouldn't have known this had I not spent the night with Cathy, but through the course of our conversation later that night, I realized that she and Stacy had met.

I don't know how on earth I managed to keep Stacy away from the house that evening. I can't even remember the lie that I used, but lying comes pretty natural to me, so I'm sure it was a pretty good one. After the event and the party following the event, Cathy came over at around 2:20 a.m.

I remember opening the door, giving her a huge fake hug, a kiss on the cheek, and making the mental note that she was wearing too much make-up. Then I asked her, "Hey babe, how was the party?"

Of course, she was excited to inform me of all of the wealthy black doctors, business people, and corporate heads in attendance. She rattled on and on about who was there, what they were wearing, how much she estimated their net worth to be, and any gossip she had on any of them. Though annoying indeed, I was able to amuse myself by pretending that her voice sounded like the adults on Charlie Brown. Keeping direct eye contact with Cathy and with a smile on my face, I continued nodding favorably as

Cathy spoke, while in my mind I heard nothing other than a rhythmic cadence of gargled mumbling. The shit was pretty funny at first. Then she caught my attention when she made mention to an interesting new friend she had met.

"I met a pretty cool sista' this evening, and she thought it may be cool for us to hang out with her and her boyfriend one weekend when I'm in town."

I'm not too big on double dating, but I figured with Cathy living out of town, I could agree to this now and make up an excuse when needed. Therefore, I agreed to do so. Cathy continued speaking.

"Anyway baby, she graduated from Stanford, she was sitting in VIP, and she was wearing a Chanel evening gown. Do you know how much that dress probably cost? Those are the type of people we need to start networking with."

At this point, I realized that her new friend was Stacy, and the double date she was referring to was her and I going out with me and Stacy. How odd was that: Stacy wanted to meet Cathy's man and Cathy wanted to meet Stacy's man. Little did they know that they already knew each beau quite well - because Cathy's man and Stacy's man was one person in the same. How my name never came up is still a mystery to me. To make things worse, they had exchanged numbers and were planning on keeping in touch.

There was no way that I could live under this type of stress, but at the same time, I couldn't figure out how to correct it. Instead, I just continued to play along.

"What's the young ladies name, Cathy?"

I already knew the answer, but I kept my cool and acted unconcerned as she nonchalantly answered my question.

"Her name is Stacy," she replied.

"Really, and what does she do for a living?" I asked.

"I don't know," she responded, then continued speaking. "But whatever it is she can afford to wear Chanel."

Suddenly, I felt relieved to know that they didn't get on the subject of accounting. Had this taken place, I would've been busted for certain. In Wichita, Kansas, there are only a handful of black CPA's, and I know my name would've come up had the conversation gone there. I continued to play my role to see if I could uncover what Cathy did and didn't know.

"I know a couple of Stacy's; what's her last name?"

Again relieved, she didn't have Stacy's last name either. I knew what needed to be asked next, but I was afraid to ask it, so I mustered up a fake laugh and blurted out other pleasantries in order to stall.

"You don't know nothing 'bout the girl except for the fact that she was wearing an expensive dress. Ewww baby, you are so crazy! She sounds cool, but you didn't get any of her information." Cathy laughed along with me, and then when she was a bit off guard, I finally spit it out.

"What's her boyfriends' name? Did you even get that?"

With a slightly embarrassed smile on her face, she looked at me, held her head down, and said, "I don't have a clue babe... I was so caught up in that dress that I don't think we discussed much else. That's bad, huh?"

I pretended to be amused by Cathy, but in actuality I was relieved to know that my name didn't come up. After all of that, I was totally out of the mood to do anything intimate with Cathy. As I was searching my mind for an excuse to get me off the hook from having to make love to Cathy, she chimed in with words that sounded like sweet music to my ears.

"Well Cameron, I hope you aren't mad at me, but I started my period today, so we can't do anything."

I assured her that I wasn't upset; I then used the excuse that I needed to be at the office early the next morning. I had already planned on going in at ten o'clock Saturday morning, but the desire to rid myself of Cathy had prompted a change of plans. By the time 7:00 a.m. came, I had woke up, endured a rather boring display of oral sex from Cathy, showered, gotten dressed, and was getting Cathy the hell out of my house. By 7:30 a.m., I was at the office.

On Saturday, I worked all day on assignments for Mr. Wilkens. For the first time ever, I had made substantial progress without any interruptions. Through my work for Wilkens, I stumbled across something quite interesting. It appeared that the company Mr. Wilkens was purchasing had reported a profit that in actuality didn't exist. Without going into the detail of an entry level accounting class, I'll just say that some expenses were hidden, which made the company appear profitable when in actuality, no profit existed.

This is something that I should have caught within the first few days of receiving these files, so I was torn between the dilemmas of informing Mr. Wilkens, or pretending not to notice. After contemplating for a while, I made a foolish decision and intentionally overlooked the misstated earnings. With the merger just around the corner, I would've surely gotten my ass ripped for just now catching this. Had I been on top of my game, I would've discovered this the first week that I was assigned the project. Therefore, I continued to prepare my reports for Wilkens and his board as if there were nothing to be alarmed about.

By the time four o'clock came around, I had worked all day without taking time out for a lunch break. I was hungry, exhausted, and sick of looking at numbers, so I decided to call it a day. I felt relieved that I was making headway on the project, so I thought I'd treat myself to a nice dinner and a few early evening cocktails.

I left the office, drove to a nearby eatery, and enjoyed a KC strip cooked medium well, along with a baked potato, a Caesar Salad, and two glasses of scotch on the rocks.

For the first time in weeks I was able to enjoy a moment of peace and solidarity. The cell phone wasn't ringing, I had gotten some work done, and at least for a moment, I wasn't consumed with the complex juggling act that comes with indulging in multiple love interests.

I finished my meal, ordered one final drink, and reflected on my day. For the most part, this was a good day. In fact, this was indeed the first good day that I had experienced in quite a while.

CHAPTER THIRTEEN
LIAR LIAR

Monday seemed to come too soon, especially after working worked all day Saturday and a few hours on Sunday. The date was August 9th 2004, and like most summer days in Kansas, the weather was strange and unpredictable. All weekend long it had been sunny and warm, but on Monday, the sky was dark and it had rained most of the day. Of course, the day's gloominess would be mild in comparison to the turmoil that fate had in store for me.

Like most Monday's, I arrived to work late after stopping at Janie's for my Monday morning service call. The Monday sessions with Janie had been going on for close to a month now, and on this particular Monday I would discover that Janie actually had a boyfriend the entire time we had been enjoying our Monday sessions. I didn't really care whether she had a guy or not, I just found this to be interesting. He had come over that morning while I was there, and she casually introduced me as her father's accountant and him as her boyfriend. I didn't get his real name at that time, but she introduced him simply as G.

I had seen G around before. If I'm not mistaken, I believe he's part of a local band that does a lot of gigs around town. Obviously, Janie has a thing for black men. G was about 6 foot tall, muscular built, and wore a short afro. He slightly resembled Malcolm Jamal Warner, so immediately after he left, I began to jokingly refer to him as Theo Huxtable. Anyway, after introducing me as the family accountant, Janie kissed Theo goodbye and was practically undressed before he had gotten out of the driveway.

After putting in work on Janie, I showered and headed out the door. I arrived at the office at around 11ish. Before I could even get situated, Mr. Underhill was calling my extension, requesting my presence in his office. I immediately left my office and went to see him. As I walked into the office, Mr. Underhill was engaged in a phone call.

"Cameron, have a seat. I'll be with you in a moment."

I sat patiently while he was finishing up his conversation with whoever it was on the other line. A few minutes later, he hung up the phone and asked me to close the office door.

"Get that door for me if you don't mind son."

I closed the door and returned to my seat.

"Hey Mr. Underhill, how's everything going?" I asked.

"Well son, I was actually about to ask you the exact same thing. How are you these days?"

"Oh, I've been doing pretty well. Just working hard trying to make these deadlines."

"I see," he said. "So tell me Cameron, how's everything going with Wilkens? I notice you've been spending a lot of time out of the office on that project. Is everything coming along alright?"

"Oh yeah. Everything is fine. I should be tying all the loose ends together here shortly."

Up to that point, I hadn't quite figured out why Mr. Underhill had summoned me, but he continued to probe.

"So how's everything with you and Stacy?"

"Everything is good with us sir. She probably wishes I wasn't putting in so much work, but everything is good." I said in a laughing tone.

Underhill's face displayed an evil smirk, and he continued speaking while nodding his head in a facetious manner.

"Good... Good. Glad to see that everything is going well with you youngsters. Yes sir! That's quite alright."

I smiled and nodded in unison with him, but still I felt a slight discomfort as my gut instinct was telling me that there was more to this conversation than just an exchange of pleasantries. Still, he continued asking strange questions and making vague statements. After a few minutes of this, the uneasiness of his probing began to escalate. Then out of the blue he blurted out a question that totally threw me for a loop.

"Yeah Cameron, that Janie is something else, huh son?"

I wasn't sure where this was going, so I tried to play it off in a manner that was both professional and politically correct. With a nervous smile on my face and a deliberate chuckle in my voice, I responded, "I don't really know too much about her, but she seems friendly enough."

"Yeah, I've known Janie since she was about 9 or 10 years old," he said.

"Like I said before, I haven't really talked to her much, but I've seen her on a few of the occasions that I've retrieved files from their house." I replied.

"Oh yeah... that's right son. You go over there to work on accounting stuff, right?"

I could tell that Mr. Underhill had a motive of some sort. At this point, I wasn't quite sure, but he seemed to be implying a possible connection between Janie and me. I thought for sure that there was no way he could've known about the Monday Special, but he seemed to suspect something. I figured I'd better tell him about Janie's boyfriend just in case he did suspect something between us.

"Janie's boyfriend seems like a nice enough fellow. I met him this morning while I was there. Have you ever met him sir? His name is G. I think he's a musician or something."

Mr. Underhill knew G, but seemed surprised that I knew him. The fact that he was there this morning seemed to remove the idea that I had been there for any non work-related purposes. Mr. Underhill paused and he proceeded in answering my question.

"I know Gerald quite well. He plays the organ at the church some sometimes. In fact, he played just last Sunday."

This was the first time G's real name had been revealed to me. I didn't let Mr. Underhill know that though. Instead, I nodded my head in agreement and kept the conversation going.

"Oh okay, I didn't know that. So, he must be pretty good, huh?"

For a brief moment, I felt relieved. I convinced myself that Underhill's implication of my involvement with Janie was just my imagination. I thought that he certainly wouldn't expect her to introduce me to G if I were there for some type of foolishness other than business. Of course, he didn't reach his level of success by being naïve, so he continued probing.

"Now Cameron, I've been in this field for a total of 30 years now, and this so called 'field work' that you've been doing is something new to me. Of course, there have been times that have required my presence at the home of clients, but every Monday morning. I don't know son, I just find that a bit odd."

I interrupted him so that I could defend myself against his implied allegations.

"Mr. Underhill, my work should speak for itself. You chose me for this project because I'm good at what I do, right?"

He scrunched up his face, turned his lips up, and replied, "Oh yeah... you are damn good at what you do. Damn good." He burst out in an evil expression of laughter and said it once again. "Yeah boy, you are good!"

Just then, I thought that he was about to let me off the hook, when he asked a question that threw my completely off guard.

"Hey Cameron, tell me what you think about my haircut. You like it?"

With a look of bewilderment on my face and in a confusing tone, I reluctantly answered his odd question while wondering about his angle, purpose, and intent for asking it.

"Uhhh yeah, your cut looks nice."

"I was hoping you'd like it. I went to see that barber you recommended a while ago."

For the life of me, I had no idea what he was talking about, but I remained silent, while maintaining the puzzled look that occupied my face. Mr. Underhill resumed speaking.

"You remember referring me to my new barber don't you Cameron?"

"No sir. I don't have a clue what you're talking about."

"Sure you do. I thought I'd go over on 13th and check out the barbershop you told me about. You do remember telling me about that shop, right?"

Suddenly, I recalled the lie I'd told him several weeks ago about me having a fight with Stacy's ex-fiancé, Logan. I hoped that he hadn't mentioned me, but I would soon discover that I couldn't expect to be so lucky. I grew a bit nervous as Mr. Underhill continued his conversation.

"You know, I think I'll make that my new barbershop. Old Todd and Will took real good care of me down there."

"Yeah, they both do a good job sir. Which one of them cut you up?"

"Well Cameron, that's the funniest part of the story. I had Todd cut my hair and Will trimmed my beard, so I spent time with both of them. Really well mannered young men. Yes indeed."

"Yeah, both of em' are good people."

"That's not the funny part though. The funny part to all of this is that neither of them seems to recall seeing you in quite some time."

"You asked about me?"

"Oh yeah, I asked about you. What's my man's name again? My new barber?"

I responded to his somewhat sarcastic question, with a question of my own.

"Are you talking about Todd?"

"That's him, Todd. Yeah Cameron, Todd says that he hasn't seen you in over a year. Maybe he was just off that day that you had the fight with Logan though, right? But wait… Will hasn't seen you either, has he Cameron?"

I attempted to speak, but he interrupted me. This time he raised his voice and pounded his fist on his desk as he spoke.

"Cameron, you know why no one saw you at the 13th Street Shop? Huh Cameron, you know why? Huh boy, do you know why? I'll tell you why Cameron, because you haven't been there!"

Things seemed as if they couldn't have been much worse at that point. My boss, whose daughter I just so happened to be fucking, was suspicious of me sleeping with the daughter of one of his clients. Plus he had also just busted me cold in a lie that I had told him nearly three weeks ago. To top all of this off, the man who had previously had so much respect for me had now discovered that I was, in actuality full of shit.

After angrily pounding on his desk and exposing me as a liar, the two of us sat still with our eyes locked together and our facial expressions motionless. For about 15 seconds, you could've heard a pin drop in his office, as the discomfort of our brief silence was intensified by my cramping stomach. I had to pass gas something awful, but didn't want to add insult to injury, so I concentrated on holding it in while withstanding Mr. Underhill's mental torture.

The uncomfortable face off between the two of us lasted about two minutes, but it felt like hours. The palms of my hands grew sweaty and my stomach pain became more intense. I refused to blink my eyes or bow my head, so a burning sensation in my eyes further increased my discomfort. My intention was to convince Mr. Underhill that he failed to intimidate me. Whether my act fooled him or not, the truth of the matter was that I was scared shitless.

Finally, my stomach muscles could no longer contain the noxious outbreak of gas I had been fighting to hold back. As I maintained eye contact with him, an awful and hideous odor silently escaped my tensely cringed body. A smell resembling that of week old rotten eggs, high octane gasoline and spoiled milk quietly occupied the air that separated the two of us.

Mr. Underhill pretended to ignore the ghastly odor, but there's no way the horrific and air contaminating odor didn't bother him. Even as the proponent of the atrocious smell, I too began to feel nauseated and dizzy by the unbearable fragrance.

Finally, the two-minute torture ended, as Mr. Underhill broke the silence with an outburst of hysterical laughter.

"Ha Ha Ha…. Boy does it smell like shit in here!"

For a brief moment, I displayed a faint smile and attempted to laugh along with him, but his next series of words silenced me again. This time, with the vigor of Samuel Jackson in one of his climatic scenes, Mr. Underhill continued.

"Yeah, it really smells like shit. Not just now, but from the time you walked into this office, all I've smelled has been a bunch of bold and italicized, hyphenated and underlined, BULLSHIT! A freshly cooked batch of stirred up, seasoned, well blended, and highlighted BULLSHIT! Do you smell it Cameron? Huh son, do you smell it?

"No sir, I can't say that I smell it."

"Oh yeah boy, you smell it! It's all over the place. You gotta smell it boy! The way you make excuses, the time you spend out of the office, the funny little story about a fight that no one else seems to know about. You can't smell all the shit in the air?"

I wanted badly to say something, but couldn't quite find anything worthwhile to speak about. As I sat still, he finally brought his brutal and grueling session to a close.

Cameron Banks... The Reality Show

"Cameron Banks, I'm sick of smelling shit today son. I need for you to get the fuck out of my office, but before you do that, I need you to understand something."

Like a six year old being caught red-handed with both hands in the cookie jar, I focused my feeble and guilt ridden eyes towards his face. His abrasive and punishing voice shifted to a soft and calculated whisper.

"Look here man; I don't know what kind of game it is that you might be trying to run here, but I need to let you know that you are real close to fucking up. If you screw up this deal with Wilkens, I'll make sure that you never get a job this side of the Mason-Dixon again. If you do anything at all to hurt Stacy; and nigga I do mean anything - so help me God, I swear to you that keeping a job will be the least of your worries. Now get the fuck out of my office before I get ugly."

I picked up my ego, crammed it into my back pocket, and walked solemnly out of Mr. Underhill's office. As I headed back to my office, I felt as if everyone was watching, whispering, and gossiping. This wasn't the case of course, but my own insecurities had gotten the best of me at that moment.

I spent the remainder of my day hiding safely behind the door to my office. Uneasy about making eye contact with any of my co-workers, I waited for everyone else to leave before finally coming out the office. By the time I was finally leaving, the clock read 6:27 p.m. As I was making my way to the front door, Mr. Underhill was returning to the office through the same door. Apparently he had forgotten something when he had left earlier. The two of us walked right passed one another without speaking and continued in that manner for the next few days. I had been conniving, gaming, and bullshittin' everyone around me, and Mr. Underhill had exposed me. A man who was ready for me to become his son in law just weeks before, now viewed me as a lying, worthless piece of shit. I knew that the only way to win at least a portion of his respect back was to deliver stellar work for Wilkens and Associates. I guess the only good thing that came out of all of this is that while tucked away in my office, I was able to complete a decent rough draft of all of the reports that needed to be presented to Wilkens.

CHAPTER FOURTEEN
Double Trouble

When I was a kid, my parents played a lot of music around the house. In fact, it wasn't the least bit uncommon for my old man to sing along with some of his favorite records. Honestly speaking, I can't say that I've ever heard a more horrible voice than his, but he was still somewhat entertaining to watch. I'm certain he knew that keeping his day job was an absolute necessity; at the same time, at any given moment during the weekends, he was usually about three glasses of bourbon and a cheap cigar away from being in concert. My younger brother, Lance, and I would laugh hysterically at pops, whose lack of musical talent was accentuated by a series of equally pathetic dance gyrations. After performing about four or five tunes, ranging in genres from Lou Rawls ballads to George Clinton funk, he'd usually end with an encore performance of an old blues song called "Double Trouble."

Cameron Banks… The Reality Show

Right off hand, I can't recall the name of the singer who had released the song "Double Trouble," but I do remember what the song was all about. The girlfriend and the wife of the artist had discovered one another, and the song discussed the dramatic dilemma between the artist and the two women referenced in the song. I don't know whether or not the song was just made up, or if the singer had really experienced such a situation. What I do know is that he described a situation that definitely wasn't good to be a part of.

On August 20th, 2004, I couldn't help but reminisce about my dad singing 'Double Trouble' loudly and out of key. On that particular day though, I didn't find the memory as funny and entertaining as I had typically found it to be. In fact, on that day, I was feeling a sense of stress similar to that of the artist who actually performed the tune.

The day was Friday, and things were relatively peaceful around the office all day. Other than a few blatantly suggestive and sexually explicit emails and calls from Stacy, I was able to work on the Wilkens account uninterrupted for most of the day.

I'm not sure what it was about Stacy on this particular Friday, but she seemed much more desirable than ever before. Perhaps it was the contrast between what she was wearing externally, and the inner-freak that I had become acquainted with.

Still as stylish as ever, for the most part, she was dressed in an overly wholesome and innocent manner. Her earth tone sundress was accented by decorative patterns of turquoise and chocolate just below her breasts. Though her high-heeled canvas sandals were from the Jimmy Choo Vintage Collection, her overall vibe was still quite conservative. Topping it off, she was wearing glasses rather than the contact lenses she typically wears, her hair was tied in a pony-tail, and I don't recall her wearing any jewelry or much make-up. Rather than a sex craved accountant with a definite type-A personality, Stacy's 'plain Jane' appearance resembled that of a librarian or a kindergarten teacher. I know the look sounds a bit boring, and I don't know why I felt the way that I did, but this look drove me insane. I guess it was because I knew that a porno star lived locked away in this image of a Sunday school teacher, and I became eager to assist Stacy with releasing her inner-freak.

After work, I stopped to purchase a fifth of Remy and headed over to Stacy's place. Before I could even get in the door, Stacy virtually attacked me. In a laughing voice, I stated, "Damn baby… let me get in the house good first."

She ignored me and continued ripping the buttons off of my shirt with both hands and her teeth. I spoke again, but my words were still ignored.

"C'mon baby, can a nigga fix a drink and get settled in first?"

She continued undressing me, and by this time, my shirt was ruined, my belt unfastened, and my fly wide open.

At that point, there was nothing left for me to do but take a few quick swallows directly from the bottle of Remy I was still holding, and join the party. By the time I had consumed the drink and screwed the top back on the bottle, my slacks and boxers were draped over my shoes, and I had been aggressively pushed onto the couch. The feeling of Stacy's gentle warm fingers and sculpted nails massaging my crouch established a nice introduction for the oral pleasures that would soon follow.

With Stacy on her knees and me sitting on the couch, I reached my hand around the back of her head and loosened the small elastic band she had used to tie her hair into a ponytail. Soon after, I began aggressively massaging her scalp with my fingers, while releasing a variety of subtle gyrations from my pelvic area. Before long, I had totally made a mess of Stacy's hair, and her appearance began to mirror that of an untamed beast. Within minutes, her beautiful, long, jet black hair went from having a smooth and organized texture to a style that Don King would envy. With hair covering her eyes and forehead, Stacy continued engaging in what was a colorful and artful act of lustfulness.

All while this was going on, I continued saying the same few words to Stacy, over and over again repeatedly, and in a seductive whisper.

"Ewwww, you so nasty Stacy! Ewww, you are sooo fuckin' nasty."

This seemed to turn Stacy on, as she'd occasionally chuckle while disagreeing.

Several times, she replied back with "Uhm uhm."

This seemed to be all that Stacy could say, as her mouth was too occupied to say much else. Still, I would continue making my statement.

"You know you nasty, don't you baby?"

Stacy released her mouth from my erect limb long enough to answer my question then resumed her erotic sexual activity.

"I'm only nasty for you daddy!" she quickly replied, then immediately placed her mouth back around my rigid organ.

After several minutes of this, I finally stood up and took off my t-shirt and shoes, and pulled my pants from around my ankles. Other than my socks, I was stark naked. Stacy was still clothed in the sundress she was wearing at work earlier, but she had apparently removed her panties during our oral encounter. I don't even remember it taking place, but her cream colored thong was somehow lying on the floor beside my feet.

Squatting towards the floor, I reached below her calves and scooped her off the ground until her body draped over my left shoulder. Walking through the house with Stacy over my shoulder, I approached the kitchen.

There were some pans and some old magazines on the kitchen counter, so I sat her on the counter, just slightly in front of these items, then used my forearm to throw all of the items from the counter onto the floor.

With Stacy now seated on the granite countertop, I slowly kneeled down until I could position my teeth on the skirt of her summer dress. With my hands slowly massaging upwards, I gently maneuvered from her ankles and calves towards her thighs and ass, all the while using my teeth to lift her skirt above her waist.

Finally, she could no longer contain her-self. She eagerly snatched the skirt from my mouth and pulled her garment around her own voluptuous ass and over her shoulders and head. Calmly, I made an attempt to lick her along the waistline and on her thighs, but she impatiently placed both of her palms firmly on the top of my head and pushed down hard, until my eyes were parallel with the moist flesh corridor residing between her full firm thighs. I allowed my tongue to penetrate and explore her insides, all while closing my eyes and fantasizing in my mind that I was Blair Underwood, engaged in a passionate tongue kiss with Jada Pinkett-Smith in the movie "Set It Off."

As I continued to pretend kissing Jada, the more involved my mouth and tongue became, and the wetter Stacy became. Soon, tasty streams of dripping erotic moisture consumed my taste buds. I could tell that Stacy was about to climax, so I continued the active contact between my tongue and her naked flesh until her legs and torso began to vibrate frantically.

Just moments prior to her achieving an orgasm, I stopped and stood to my feet so that I could be face to face with her, while she was still seated on the counter. For about 30 seconds, she looked upset that I had deprived her of the pleasure she was just about to experience. I placed my hands firmly on her ass just below the waist and lifted her body from the counter. With Stacy suspended in the air and her hands wrapped tightly around my neck, she maneuvered her lower body until I could penetrate her in a manner that appeared as artistic and statuesque as ancient stone sculptures. Within minutes, Stacy had again reached the point of pleasure she had experienced just moments prior. This time, instead of discontinuing, I hunched my back, bent my knees, and pulled her body as close as possible to mine, all while still standing upright on my feet. Stacy had just reached her sexual boiling point, and her weakened legs and hands confirmed this. No longer was she able to continue assisting me in holding her up, and her body immediately grew much heavier. The muscles in my legs began to ache tremendously, so I gently laid her body on the kitchen floor and positioned myself on top of her. This entire time, I never removed myself from being inside of her body. Moments later, she reached her first peak, followed by a second orgasm about three minutes later. The second sensation seemed far more intense than the first one, so based on her reaction I assumed I had hit the panic button. At this point, I could go on and explain the difference between a clitoral and vaginal orgasm, but rather than doing that, I'll leave such advice to experts like Dr. Ruth or Sue Johansen. Meanwhile, let me just say that everything else that took place between us is far too nasty for me to discuss.

A couple of hours later, we were lying together, naked and unashamed beneath the covers of Stacy's king-sized bed. Although I was only partially awake, the ringing of Stacy's telephone brought me back to a state of complete consciousness. My eyes were still closed, but I could hear Stacy and the very loud and intrusive voice coming through the telephone headset. Of course, I would recognize such an obnoxious voice in a heartbeat. Without question, it was Cathy on the line with her. I had totally forgotten that the two of them had exchanged numbers at the hair show back on August 6th. Plus, I didn't think they'd be keeping in touch anyway, so I hadn't really worried much about the situation. Low and behold though, here it is two weeks later, and Cathy is calling to set up a double date. During the entire phone call, I continued to pretend that I was sleeping, while the two ladies made plans.

"Hey girl, I'm in town for the weekend," Cathy said to Stacy.

"Really! Well what type of plans do you have for tomorrow night?" Stacy asked excitedly.

"Girl, none really. I thought that maybe me and my boo could hang out with you and your boyfriend and have some drinks, or go dancing or something."

"My baby and I don't have any plans, so that's cool with me if it's okay with him. I don't wanna wake him up right now though, so I'll let you know something when he wakes up."

Stacy and Cathy shared a laugh as Stacy continued speaking.

"I had to put a little sumptin-sumptin on baby, so he probably won't be waking up for a minute girl." Stacy stated with laughter in her voice.

Still pretending to be asleep, I listened to the two women laugh and joke, but never once was my name mentioned. I don't know how and why it never came up, but I thanked God it never did.

Cathy brought the conversation to an end by letting Stacy know that she needed to call her male friend to inform him that she was in town. Little did she know, but he found out at the same time that Stacy did.

As soon as the conversation between the two females finally ended, my phone started ringing. I knew this was Cathy calling, so I kept my eyes closed just enough to look sleep, but squinting to see whether or not Stacy would try to look at my phone.

Of course, she looked at me to ensure herself that I wouldn't be waking up. Then she picked up the phone to see who was calling. Fortunately, my cell phone displays the name only and not the phone number if I program a person's number under their name. Since I program all females into my phone under alias-male code names, Stacy would never figure out that this was Cathy calling me. I actually had the number programmed under the name Al McFall, so she immediately saw the name and assumed it to be a guy calling. As I expected, she looked at the call display, looked at me, then she sat my phone back down on the floor beside my pants and my mutilated shirt.

By that time, I was nervous and scatter brained. There was no way that I could commit to going on a double date, when I was the date of both parties. Finally, I got out of Stacy's bed, claiming to be headed back to the office to work on stuff for Wilkens.

After I put on my clothes, I kissed her on the cheek, and left her home at approximately 10:30 p.m.

I knew that eventually these ladies would discuss me by name and occupation, and if this were to happen, I'd be absolutely busted. This situation was just far too nerve racking for me, so I needed to react.

Since I already wasn't too fond of Cathy, I knew that it was time to remove myself from that situation. I called Cathy back from missing her call about an hour earlier and acted pleasantly surprised that she was in town for the weekend. Of course, she mentioned the double date, and of course I had to make an excuse.

"Damn Cathy! I wish you had called earlier in the week. I would've cancelled my trip had I known sooner."

"Trip? What trip?" she responded.

"I told you about my brother Lance being in prison, right? I'm going up to visit him Saturday and Sunday."

At first, I was feeling bad about the lie that I was about to tell Cathy. Then she reminded me of all of the reasons she disgusted me to begin with. Like usual, she began running her mouth without knowing what the hell she was talking about. Again I'll say that I hate using the word bitch, but the English language fails to possess a word strong enough to illustrate my resentment for Cathy. For now, bitch will have to suffice.

"Cameron, you have a college degree and a CPA license. I don't know why you still fool with Lance!"

In a concerned and sincere voice, I responded to her ridiculous statement.

"What the fuck are you talking about, he's my fuckin' brother."

"Yeah, but he's in prison. You've got to learn to cut people loose that aren't on your level."

"So if you had a brother or sister who made a mistake, it's that simple for you? You just write em' off as being worthless pieces of shit because they made a fucking mistake?"

"Absolutely!"

By then I had grown a bit angry, as I continued in this ridiculous debate.

"You've gotta be fucking kidding me, Cathy."

"I don't know Cameron, maybe we were just raised differently. Sometimes I question your values though."

"What in the fuck is that stupid ass shit supposed to mean Cathy?"

"Nothing... I'm just saying that maybe your parents didn't teach you guys the same values that my parents taught us. First off, there are five of us, all five have college degrees and none of us have ever been to jail. You've got a brother in jail, a cousin in jail and a bunch of friends that don't even have degrees. Why do you even hang out with people who aren't educated?"

By then, I was so livid that my demeanor had escalated from calm and concerned to irate and bitter. With anger and hatred in my voice, I yelled the following words into the telephone receiver.

"ARE YOU FUCKIN' RETARDED? Who in the hell told you that you need a degree in order to be educated? I know high-school drop outs with more intellectual capacity than me and you combined!"

She spoke again, this time sounding no less stupid than she had throughout the conversation, or any of our conversations for that matter.

"Well, that's just a matter of opinion Cameron. I don't see how you think that a person with a Masters degree wouldn't be smarter than a person with no degree at all. That's just silly."

Realizing that I couldn't convince this idiot that a degree only measures the discipline to complete a program, and not overall intelligence; I gave up and began making blatant and sarcastic attempts to piss her off and end our conversation.

"I'll tell you what Cathy, how 'bout you just let me touch the hem of your garment so I can be made whole! That alright with you?"

"What's that supposed to mean?" she replied in a disturbed tone.

"I mean, damn! You've got soooo many negative opinions of everyone else, yet you seem to view yourself as such the glowing image of perfection. Can you walk on water? Maybe make the blind see?"

"Look Cameron, I don't appreciate you patronizing me. Stop it right now. I mean it!"

"I'm a little thirsty this evening and the liquor store is closing soon. Perhaps you could turn a little water into wine for a nigga. A nice Merlot or a Cabernet would be great?"

By now, she is so angry that she's yelling and hollering at me through the phone. Nonetheless, I continued to instigate.

"Seeing how you heal the sick and walk on water and all, it's obvious to me, Cathy, that you must be Jesus Christ! Yes indeed... all praises due to Cathy, for she has done marvelous things! Make a joyful noise unto this bitch, shall we?"

As I was about to continue to go off, I hear the phone click. Cathy had hung up in my face and the conversation had ended. I was almost at the office, but I really didn't want to go in. I spun a U-turn in the middle of the street and headed back to Stacy's house.

For the next hour or so, I was so mad that I developed a headache and my hands were shaking.

As I pulled into Stacy's driveway, I received a text message from Cathy that said, "until you learn how to talk to me with respect Negro, don't you ever fuckin' talk to me again."

"Good riddance to bad rubbish," I thought to myself while reading Cathy's memo. Though I was still bothered by her insult of my brother and just the overall attitude that her nasty ass didn't stink, I was relieved that the argument would keep her away from me for a while - hopefully for good. My only fear was that the newfound friendship between Stacy and Cathy would continue developing. I would definitely always have to worry about my identity being revealed. Meanwhile, I was at least off the hook for the weekend.

CHAPTER FIFTEEN
Kick It Down!

===

TROUBLE

So high, you can't get over it
So low, you can't under it
So wide, you can't get around
It's time to go ahead and kick it down

Several weeks passed and the middle of September came. It was Thursday, September 16th. From the outside looking in, I'm sure that my life appeared to be a bed of milk and honey. On the inside though, I was slowly crumbling to pieces.

My project for Wilkens needed to be completed by October 15th. That was less than a month away, and I wasn't even close to being done. In addition to giving less than a half assed effort to the most important work assignment of my life, I had extended myself financially and my social life was in shambles. For starters, I was unwillingly involved in a relationship with the deranged daughter of my boss. As if this situation in itself wasn't dangerous enough, I had been using the excuse of 'field work' in order to leave the office every Monday for no other purpose than to seduce the daughter of our most important client. Add to all of this the fact that not only do these two women know one another, but their families also share a great deal of history. Top this off with the fact that Mr. Underhill had slightly caught on to my nonsense. Then there's Cathy, who I'd been involved with for a few months now as well. Since she didn't live in town, the only time I was required to deal with her was when she occasionally came to town to visit her folks. This was still a burden for the simple fact that when she came home, I'd have to create a series of lies so that no one would question my unavailability on those particular weekends. Of course, there was also the added stress of the newfound friendship that Cathy and Stacy were developing.

What made the Cathy situation even more cumbersome is that I didn't like the chic at all, so I can't figure out why I even bothered going through such an extent of trouble. Who knows, maybe I just have a hard time saying no... Perhaps I had become so vain that the flattery of being desired was something that I was incapable of resisting... at least for the time being, Cathy was still pissed off at me and we weren't on speaking terms, so that was one less headache at least for the moment. Still, even with that, I knew that there was a possibility that we'd eventually exchange the facial expressions that coincide with acts of passion and lust - those faces that the rapper Scarface describes so eloquently in his song, "Fuck Faces." Regardless as to why I allowed myself to ever become involved with Cathy; why I remained involved with her as long as I did; and why I'd consider going down that path again is a mystery even to me. One thing for certain though is that I did truly despise her and everything about her. There isn't much more that I can say in expressing my disgust for her, so I'll just end this thought by mentioning that she is truly the type of lady that gives the word 'bitch' a bad name. Then of course, there's Cheyenne and the real feelings I had for her. Amidst all the drama in her life, I had a hard time staying away from her. She hadn't been returning my calls lately, so I assumed that K-9 had her on lock down. My feelings for her were sincere and her relationship with K-9 bothered me more than slightly, but it was what it was. I wasn't in a position to be with Cheyenne and of course, she wanted a thug.

On that particular Thursday morning, the office was granted a casual day, so like most of my peers, I was wearing jeans. In the way of the rest of my attire, I wasn't dressed in anything too outlandish, but even in blue jeans I still managed to set the bar in terms of how a professional should dress. My light colored denims were heavily starched and creased with impeccable precision. My button down, long sleeved shirt was starched heavily as well, and its bright lavender and white checkered design was accented by the elegant contrast of light brown Italian loafers and a matching light brown belt. Finally, a dark brown blazer and a pair of lavender socks with brown diamond shaped designs completed the ensemble.

I arrived at the office at 5:30 a.m., and by the time everyone else arrived at 8:00 a.m., I had already been working diligently on financial statements for Mr. Wilkens. Keeping the door to my office closed, I continued working, and before I knew it, the time was 11:30 a.m. By then, I was starving.

For lunch, I had a craving for some authentic soul food, so I headed to Niecey's; a little hole in the wall restaurant in the hood.

By noon, I had been seated and my food had reached the table. My order of hot, delicious, and unhealthy high blood pressure on a platter consisted of spicy cabbage, warm buttered cornbread muffins, and tender neck bones drenched in hot sauce, black eyed peas, and fried potatoes, all to be washed down with a refreshing glass of red Kool Aid served from an old fashioned Mason jar. Niecey's restaurant doesn't have a set menu, and the variety is typically limited to just two choices that change daily, based on what two entrees the owner, Niecey, decideds to cook that day.

By 12:30 p.m., I had finished my meal, along with a very unhealthy slice of strawberry cake. I paid my tab and headed towards the door. To my surprise, when I opened the door to walk outside, Cheyenne was standing in front of the restaurant wearing a pair of stylish shades. Though I had spoken with her on the phone a few times, I hadn't seen her in several weeks, so I was initially enthused that I had run into her. I approached Cheyenne to embrace her, but she nervously pulled away from me. With a puzzled look on my face, I shrugged my shoulders in order to express my confusion with the situation.

"Damn baby... you act like you ain't ever seen me before! What's been up with you?" Cheyenne responded, but was short with her answer and still appeared to be nervous.

"Nothing, I need to go inside the restaurant." She responded.

As she spoke, something told me to reach for her shades. She resisted for a few seconds, but it didn't take long for me to get them off of her face and notice that both of her eyes were severely blackened.

While standing face to face with her, still holding her shades in my hand, K-9 walked up and approached the two of us. At first, I didn't realize that he was accompanying her. He must have been parking the car or something... who knows? Anyway, as he walked up on the two of us, he aggressively snatched her by the arm and attempted to yank her into the restaurant.

"Bitch, if you don't bring yo' punk ass," he said as he angrily grabbed her by the arm.

K-9 continued speaking to Cheyenne, but never once looked in my direction.

"I told you to stay the fuck away from that bitch ass nigga, and you still insist on making me fuck you up."

Cheyenne used her hand to cover the tears that occupied her face, so I reached out to hand her the sunglasses I was still holding. As she reached for the shades, K-9 aggressively slapped them out of my hand and they broke as they hit the concrete. At that moment, he and I looked at one another, and without saying another word, I charged him with a quick left jab followed by a stiff overhand right. Both punches connected with his face, but he still maintained enough energy and poise to lunge forward and tackle me to the ground. Fortunately, my head safely hit the patch of grass running adjacent to the sidewalk of the restaurant rather then hitting the concrete. The two of us struggled with one another until I was eventually able to flip him over to his backside. With my left hand tightly clinched against his neck, I used my right hand to repeatedly strike him in the face. Angry words escaped my mouth while I commenced to punish him.

"Nigga, you wanna kick somebody's ass? Huh nigga?"

He wasn't saying much of anything. His hands were full as he had become completely occupied with trying to break free from my grasp.

By now, I wasn't just angry that he'd attacked me, but I was equally angry at the fact that he had been physically abusive with Cheyenne. In my opinion, when a man is physically abusive with a queen, it displays insecurity, selfishness, and just overall signs of a weak ass, sorry punk ass dude. Therefore, as I continued beating K-9 in the face, it was almost as if I was attempting to punish him not just for his ill actions with Cheyenne, but for all abusive actions towards women.

He was finally able to throw me off of him, and he screamed out various vulgarities towards me as we separated and both rose to our feet.

"Fuck you nigga…" is one of many foul comments K-9 charges me with. "Come on; bring your bitch ass on nigga!"

K-9 lunged towards me once again, and this time we locked up. As he used his strength to try and maneuver forward, I grabbed a hold of his shoulders, pulled him towards me and allowed his own strength and forward momentum to assist me in easily throwing him back onto the ground.

Again, I resumed delivering a series of rapid punches to his face, while also yelling vulgarities of my own.

"Naw nigga, fuck you. You ain't getting up this time!" I yelled out as the two of us continued to engage in a physical warfare that had been totally lopsided up to that point.

Though he was now bleeding profusely, he continued trying to fight back. I never realized how much blood could be produced from a severe cut beneath the eye and a busted lip, but his already hideous face had become so drenched in blood that he resembled a pit bull that had just been defeated in a dog fight.

Somehow, K-9 was able to finally release his neck from my grasp and he grabbed the back of my head. We wrestled for a moment, until I felt a blunt object hit me in the back of the head. Cheyenne had struck me with an empty beer bottle in an effort to protect K-9. Although it hurt like hell, the cuts suffered from the broken glass were only minor in comparison to the gashes that K-9 was modeling. Even more painful than his scars or those of my own was my hurt pride, and devastated feelings. Why would Cheyenne come to the rescue of this jerk? For the life of me, I couldn't figure out. After all, part of why I was even fighting K-9 was to defend her and she apparently didn't appreciate it.

Niecey must have called for assistance with the situation, as my encounter with K-9 was obviously a distraction to her business. Two men in their early thirties pulled up. One of them was well over 6 feet tall and slender and the other was stocky, about 5'10" and looked to be a rock solid 220 if I had to guess. I'm pretty sure that these men were Niecey's nephews. Their car pulled up and both gentlemen rushed out in order to break up what, by that time wasn't much of a fight.

The larger of the two gentlemen pulled me away from K-9 and held me in order to ensure that I'd refrain from attacking him again. The other man helped K-9 to his feet and informed both of us that we needed to leave.

"Y'all can't be coming up in here disrespectin' my ant'ee business like that," the smaller of the two men said. His voice had a strong southern twang and his demeanor was forceful. Later, I heard Niecey refer to her nephews by the names of Pooh and Chubb, so you know these folks weren't from Kansas. In fact, if my memory serves me right, I think they came here from a place called Morgan City, Louisiana.

The other gentleman chimed in as well and spoke angrily and with a similar accent.

"Yeah… y'all niggas need to take dat shit on down yonder. We tryin' to run a bidness' over here!"

This was the second time that I had fought K-9, and I was hoping this wasn't about to become an ongoing event. My record against this bum was now 2 and 0, but this time it was different. During my first bout with K-9, no one was there to witness it. This time though, K-9 had his pride on the line with Cheyenne there watching the scene unfold.

After a few moments of K-9 and I exchanging evil stares while still being restrained by the two men, I looked directly at K-9, cast an evil smile, and I let out a brief laugh while walking towards my car.

Embarrassed, humiliated, and pissed, I was certain that he wouldn't be seeking revenge. That didn't stop him from talking shit though.

"Oh, nigga it's on when I see you. On everything I love nigga, it's on." He yelled while I continued to walk away laughing on the outside, but emotionally scarred within.

Honestly speaking, K-9's threats didn't bother me at all. What did disturb me was that Cheyenne was there for him. She had already attacked me in his defense. After the fight, she stood there brushing the grass off his clothes and hair and holding tightly to his arm to show her support. I can't lie; seeing that shit hurt me much more than the cut on my head.

I left the premises and went home to clean up, then dressed the wound that Cheyenne's bottle had left on my head, and changed clothes.

I arrived back at the office at three o'clock. I was still swamped with work to do for Wilkens, so my intention was to work until seven.

Unfortunately for me, I was unable to get much done. Every 15 to 20 minutes, Stacy would call me or send me emails wanting to talk about us. Though I continued begging her to let me get some work done, she just couldn't seem to refrain from asking me a series of annoying ass questions:

"Are you seeing someone else?" "Do you still want to be with me?" "We need to talk about us!!" "You've seemed distant lately!" "Are you sure you still want this?"

By the time five o'clock had arrived, I hadn't done much of anything other than communicate with Stacy about things that I felt could wait. The whole scene had me so frustrated that combined with the fight I had earlier, I was too tired and frustrated to do much of anything, so rather than working late, I left the office and headed home.

CHAPTER SIXTEEN
The Boiler Room

The last three to four weeks leading up to October 15th were possibly the most mentally challenging weeks of my entire life. Even after my horrible confrontation with Mr. Underhill, lust seemed to outweigh logic and I was still foolishly involved with Janie. Most Monday mornings still consisted of me stopping by and watching Janie kiss Theo Huxtable goodbye. I'd usually shake Theo's hand and wish him a great day, and then his special lady friend and I would engage in a wild and unadulterated exchange of uninhibited grown folk activities.

In addition to this, Stacy still required an abundance of attention throughout the week. Fortunately, she was a bit more naïve than her daddy, so she never suspected much during my Monday morning office escapes.

If the drama of entertaining these two women wasn't enough to keep me occupied, I had also allowed Cathy to casually maneuver herself back into my good graces. By the way, did I mention how much I despised and still despise Cathy? In case I didn't mention this enough already, let me say it again. If nothing else, at least this illustrates just how much I enjoyed abusing myself.

Fully aware of all of the stress and headaches that juggling several women was causing me, I still had yet to do something about the situation. My work and my overall mental state were beginning to suffer; yet I continued allowing my personal life to grow deeper and deeper out of control. Furthermore, my financial situation was getting out of control too. Though I was making well over $100,000 per year, I seemed to be spending it as if it had an expiration date. I won't go too deep into my personal finances, but I will say that it doesn't take much to get a person behind the 8-ball. Maxed out credit cards, three car payments, a motorcycle loan, a loan for designer furniture, student loan payments, and a variety of other useless expenses seemed to pile up to the point that I found myself barely making it from paycheck to paycheck. Hell, I hadn't made an insurance payment on my BMW in nearly three months. Nonetheless, I guess my dad was right when he referred to me as 'the last of the big spenders'. Indeed, I was. But to those who didn't know any better, I appeared to be as confident and graceful as Jordan in Game 7. One thing was certain though, no matter how easy the task of fooling others became, every gaze in the mirror would bring me face to face with the reflection of the one individual I could never fool.

With all of these things taking place, I still found time to get everything prepared for my meeting with Wilkens. From September 16th to October 13th, I worked until at least midnight every night, and on the 14th, I pretty much pulled an all-nighter. I literally worked until 6:30 a.m. and arrived at the office at 7:45. By the time I had reviewed my notes and PowerPoint slides, it was 8:15 a.m. The meeting started promptly at 8:30 a.m.

The meeting consisted of 11 people. For starters, there was Mr. Underhill and his partner,

Shelton Crabtree. Shelton's father was actually the founder of the firm. Also present was Wilkens, and a group of five Lebanese investors. Then you had me, the principal CPA who had prepared all of the financial documents. Also present were two of the firms' newest accountants, who had assisted me with some of the legwork.

The whole deal in a nutshell was this: Wilkens is a mogul in every sense of the word, with a reputation for acquiring and selling companies. Though his company was privately owned, this deal involved his firm purchasing a public organization five times the size of his organization; then making that firm private. My job was to review all of the holdings of the company being purchased and all of the financial statements, then either inform Mr. Wilkens' Board of the reasons why this wouldn't be a wise purchase, or demonstrate why this purchase would prove to be a profitable venture – merely from a numbers standpoint. In all honesty, I fucked around and missed the August 1st deadline for reporting any red flags and blatant reasons that the venture may have been non-feasible. Since I hadn't been on top of my game, I didn't detect any potential issues until August 6th. Therefore, to cover my ass, I was balls to the walls on doing my part to get this deal done and hiding the fact that there were some questionable affairs surrounding the deal.

Mr. Underhill began the meeting by introducing all of the parties to one another, then introducing me. Though his introduction of me was probably no longer than a minute, my nerves were getting the best of me, which made his brief intro appear longer than it actually was. He finally ended and turned the floor over to me.

"Cameron is one of the brightest young accountants I've ever seen, and we know you'll be pleased with his work, just as all of the clients have been that he's worked with!"

Though I was tired, quite nervous, and more than slightly unprepared, I hoped to be able to live up to the praise and acclaim that Underhill had given me. Slowly, I began speaking.

"Good Morning ladies and gentlemen! Let me start by saying that of all of the firms you could've chosen to handle your needs, we are quite thankful that you chose Wallace, Underhill and Crabtree, and we're quite confident that you won't be disappointed with the level of service we plan on providing you."

I take it that my introduction was well taken. Everyone in the room seemed to smile and nod their heads in approval. Of course, my attire may have assisted my approval rating as well. The blue pinstripes on my light brown Paz Zileri suit alone made an impressive statement. To take the look over the top, my suit was complemented by a Hershey Chocolate bow-tie and heavily starched beige shirt, and my shoes were ivory cracked white leather Carlo Ventura loafers. Finally, wire framed Ralph Lauren non-prescription eyeglasses added a slight spark of intellect and credibility.

I definitely looked the part of excellence, and was hoping that I could speak it as well. For the next three hours, I went through various reports, explained different line items, and answered several questions.

By the time the meeting ended at noon, everyone agreed that I had done one hell of a job. Wilkens and his investors would likely be moving on with the acquisition, and our firm would continue to be paid handsomely through each phase of the process. Somehow I had managed to pull it off, and as long as my little secret didn't get out, I would be well on my way to again being the superstar of the firm. Things had been tense between me and Underhill ever since our small incident. Hopefully, today's performance would catapult back into his good graces.

CHAPTER SEVENTEEN
Caught Up...

Settle down sit back here the story goes
Listen to me while I break downa'
young playas' woes
About two cognacs and a beer ago
I was trippin' off some shit that happened
bout a year ago...

As I sat, after consuming two shots of Remy and an ice cold Modelo, I couldn't help but reminisce about what happened on Saturday, October 30th, 2004.

Things seemed to be getting better with Mr. Underhill. In fact, by the end of the day on Friday, we were even back on speaking terms. Though I won't go as far as saying that I had returned to being his hero, I do know that he was impressed with how I handled the Wilkens' meeting.

Like most weekends, this one was also uneventful. With the first phase of my work for

Wilkens done, I finally had some time to collect my thoughts and breathe again. I spent all day that Saturday with Stacy, and after visiting the mall and having lunch, we found ourselves back at my place. Since neither of us had much to do or anywhere to be, we decided to make pineapple martinis and watch television to occupy our time. After a few minutes of channel surfing, I was pleasantly surprised to see that *The Mack* was being broadcast on one of the nostalgic movie channels.

This particular urban classic was released in the early 70's and starred Max Julian and Richard Pryor. Julian portrayed a slick and street savvy pimp named Goldy, who pursues the classic American rags to riches dream through the business of illegal solicitation, while Pryor's character 'Slim' served as Julian's hype man, confidant and comic sidekick.

My dad often jokingly referred to this flick, claiming it had ruined an entire generation of good black men. In fact, his exact words went as such:

"Man, when that movie came out, niggas lost they goddamn minds."

Laughingly, he would continue - "Niggas was buying Cadillac Deville's, quitting good jobs, leaving families, and trying to be like that damn Goldy! I'll be damn."

I had seen the flick close to a dozen times already, so I reached for the remote in order to turn the channel. Apparently though, Stacy was fascinated by her first time witnessing this or any other black exploitation film for that matter.

"Wait Cam... don't turn it yet. Let's watch this for a minute. Oh my God. This is sooooo funny."

As we continued watching *The Mack*, she became increasingly fascinated with the attire and jargon of the colorful and charismatic characters. Pimps in bright colored suits and velvet hats wore shoulder length perms and referred to one another as "macks" and to their lady counterparts as "bitches" and "hos". Those individuals unfamiliar with this unique microcosm of a world were referred to as 'tricks' and 'squares'. Out of all of this, the scene that seemed to take Stacy over the top was Goldie receiving "Pimp of the Year" honors at the annual player's ball.

As we continued watching, we consumed one refreshing martini after the other, until both of us went from being slightly tipsy to outright drunk. In her state of intoxication, she suggested that we role-play and pretend to be the characters in the film.

At first I was reluctant, but after a while this became pretty amusing. In fact, what started as a playful imitation of characters in a movie eventually became a full-fledged sex-capade, complete with all of the jargon, attitude, and mentality of the movie.

In real life, Stacy would never in a million years even dream of calling me daddy, and God only knows if I were to ever call her a bitch, I'd also be calling an ambulance. In today's warped role-play though, this was acceptable. In fact, it even went as far as Stacy referring to herself in a derogatory manner as the role-playing continued.

Comments like "Daddy, I wanna be a good ho for you" and questions such as "Am I your best bitch daddy?" seemed to roll naturally off of her tongue.

I'm embarrassed to admit this, but not only was I enjoying it; but from time to time, I think I forgot that this shit wasn't real.

By the time we finished drinking, watching the movie, role playing, and enjoying a rather demented sexual encounter, the last thing I recalled was rolling over and nodding off at around 7:00 p.m. For a couple of hours, I slept like a baby as I assumed that all was peaceful and well between the two of us.

Then at around 9:15 p.m., the sound of Stacy's voice abruptly awakened me, piercing through my unconsciousness with a discomfort similar to that of a sharp object piercing human flesh.

"You dirty Mutha' Fucka' - you dirty ass, filthy, no good Mutha' Fucka! You sorry ass, dirty, piece of shit ass Mutha' Fucka you! HOW COULD YOU?"

Stacy continued getting louder and more emotional as she continued chanting the same monotonous chorus. Still partially asleep and not too alarmed, I contemplated how to explain the phone bills, hotel receipts, and even the ladies lingerie lying on the bed. She had definitely been going through my stuff, so my plan was to simply come up with a brilliant lie, then make her feel bad about nosing through my personal belongings.

Suddenly, a slap across the side of my face awakened me fully, and her angry voice drowned in the distance as the images of propaganda lying on the bed became blurry. Even the stinging sensation from her violent expression would last just momentarily, as everything taking place became upstaged by the fact that she was playing the video tape that I had made with Janie. As I focused on the television set, my eyes widened and my jaws dropped, as I had become overtaken by amazement and disbelief.

I remember it like it just happened this morning. Stacy was naked underneath my white terry cloth shower robe, and her nostrils were flaring like that of an angry and untamed wild beast. Tears filled her eyes as well, as she continued repeatedly referring to me as different variations of the same theme - "no good, dirty mother fuckers."

Stacy continued slapping me repeatedly, while expressing her utter disbelief that I would be dirty enough to cheat with "this white bitch" as she referred to Janie.

No lie I could conjure up would explain this, so I remained silent, desperately seeking the right words. A faint dizziness came over me, as Stacy continued cursing me, and violently attacking me.

She had obviously gone through my drawers while I was asleep, and had come across an old cell phone bill, some hotel receipts and of course, this videotape which I had foolishly labeled "FREAKY TALES - the tape that Janie and I had made during one of our Monday morning exploits.

After cutting my face with her nails, hitting me in the head with a K-Swiss tennis shoe, throwing a martini glass and several DVD movies towards me, knocking everything off of my dresser and breaking most of the glasses from my shot glass collection, Stacy momentarily calmed down just enough for me to grab hold of her by the arms in order to contain her and to keep her from destroying my home.

At the top of her lungs, she resumed screaming while attempting to escape my firm grasp.

"Let me go you bitch ass nigga!!!"

Without saying a word, I maintained a firm grasp of her arms.

"You fuckin' punk ass, no good, cheatin' ass, bitch ass nigga. FUCK YOU CAMERON! FUCK YOU!"

She continued yelling angry obscenities, but her resistance weakened as she became tired. Finally, she stopped resisting all together, and her screaming rage transitioned to an irritating whimper, similar to that of a kitten when being aggressively tugged by its tail.

Like untamed rapids, tears continued pouring along the side of her disturbed face. Unsure as to whether or not it was safe to do so, I reluctantly released her from my grasp.

I could feel an irritable sensation just below my eye, so I rubbed my face in that area, and as I had thought, I was slightly bleeding. Throughout all of the commotion, I must have also bit my bottom lip, which was also bleeding.

Stacy looked at me, and this time in a quiet and tearful voice, she continued demanding an answer, as over and over again, she continued asking, "Why?"

"Why, Cameron? Why? Why? Why?" she continued to cry out.

Still unable to speak, I just continued listening; afraid to utter a word while Stacy went through the full range of emotions accompanying the pain that I had caused her.

After several hours of drama, turmoil, and passionate anger, I still hadn't uttered a single word. Stacy was crazy enough without being given a reason to be, so I knew that I was treading on shaky ground with this situation. Therefore, I chose not to explain, complain, or apologize, as I remained quiet while she traveled through a maze of unstable emotional tirades. Still she persisted in trying to make me speak.

"This is sooo fucked up Cameron. You ain't got shit to say? I can't believe it. This nigga ain't got a motherfuckin' word to say. You hear me talking to you Cameron? Huh? You hear me? You ain't got shit to say nigga? Nothin?"

Finally, at midnight, she demanded that I take her home. I attempted to hand her some of her things, but she snatched her pants away from me and in an angry fashion, began rapidly dressing herself. By the time I threw on my sweatshirt, Stacy was fully dressed and ready to go. As we headed towards the front door, both of us were in complete silence, but she would occasionally look at me in a manner exhibiting such disgust that I'm certain she'd just assume I were dead.

As we approached the car, I attempted to open Stacy's door, but she slapped my hand away from the door handle and damn near slammed my hand in the car door as she briskly jumped into the car and slammed the door behind her.

I walked slowly around to the driver's side, got in the car, started the engine, backed out of the driveway, and headed towards her house as I pondered the nights incident in disbelief.

As we headed towards her place, both of us remained silent. I wondered what she was thinking, so I contemplated asking her, but opted not to. Meanwhile, it appeared that my lies and games had gotten the best of me. The whole scene made me think about Denzel Washington in "Out of Time". Although it's hard to feel sorry for a man with a wife played by Eva Mendez and Sanaa Lathan as his mistress, I have to admit that I truly found myself rooting for ole' Denzel as he struggled throughout the movie to cover up one series of lies after the next. Though I'm slightly ashamed to admit this and perhaps a bit chauvinistic for saying it; whatever the case, be it good or bad, I remember talking to the television while coaching Denzel on what lie to say next. By the time the heat had cooled down and it appeared that everything was going to turn out alright for him; I even remember releasing a sigh of relief while thinking to myself, "we did it" as he had eventually maneuvered his way out of the series of messy situations his dual life had gotten him caught up in. Unfortunately for me, my situation with Stacy

Cameron Banks... The Reality Show was real life and not a scripted series of words and actions set to film. Unlike Denzel, I didn't have a prewritten happy ending or fans cheering me to victory. Unfortunately for me, I had found myself in a situation that allowed only one take, with no room for rehearsal, cuts or edits, and I must say that this was a bad take. As smooth as I had always prided myself on being, I had found myself in a situation in which I was truly caught up.

CHAPTER EIGHTEEN
Never Seen a Man Cry

Although driving Stacy home took no more than 15 minutes, the trip felt as endless as a road trip with the Griswald Family. Upon arriving at her place, the two of us sat in the car in complete silence. After a few minutes of this, she finally spoke in a tearful voice.

"Can you come inside for a minute?"

At this point, all I could think about was joining Sam Cooke and Al Green. I won't go into detail about the Cooke story for those unfamiliar with it, but I will say that it probably isn't wise to fall asleep in the presence of a scorned woman. Of course in Al's case, it didn't turn out too good for the woman. Despite all of this, I reluctantly got out of the car and escorted Stacy into her home.

Everything seemed to be moving in a surreal sense of slow motion, as I hopelessly waited for someone to pinch me and awaken me from this awful dream. Of course, this never happened, as I was left staring face to face with my irresponsible actions.

Even though these were probably some of the worst moments I can recall, I can honestly say that I don't regret the actions that led to that moment; I only regret getting caught. If I had it to do all over again, I can't say that I wouldn't. The only thing that I can say with 100% certainty is that I'd definitely approach the situation differently.

All sorts of thoughts ran wild through my head as Stacy and I sat on the side of her bed. Previously, I hadn't mentioned that I possess a mild sleeping disorder, and I've been known to occasionally doze off unexpectedly. At 1:30 a.m., I started nodding off, but I fought hard and managed to stay awake. Here it was early Halloween morning, and I was nodding off in the presence of an angry, scorned, and potentially dangerous lady. Not the wisest thing to do, right?

Meanwhile, Stacy and I continued our discussion. By this time, trying to conjure up a believable story had exhausted me. She had found receipts from local hotels dated for days that I had claimed to be out of town and she'd found an old cell phone bill detailing several questionable calls. As I stated previously, she'd even found a pair of Cheyenne's panties. But the ultimate nail in the coffin though, was that damn videotape.

I thought about using the 'it wasn't me approach' and blaming it on my younger brother Lance, but he's in prison and Stacy already knew that. Besides, the two of us may resemble, but not enough to pull that off. I even thought about saying that this took place years ago, but that excuse was negated by the time stamp on the video, coupled with the fact that Stacy was present when Janie and I met at her mom and dad's dinner party.

Finally, at 1:45 a.m., I decided to man up and face the consequences of my actions. After having little to nothing to say for the past couple of hours, I finally spoke up and discussed my actions with Stacy.

"Stacy, I know you're wondering how and why I could do something like this."

With a look of pure disgust on her face, she looked me in the eyes, eagerly awaiting me to continue speaking, so I did.

"Anyway Stacy, I know you probably feel betrayed and perhaps even a bit misused. I can't blame you for feeling like that. All I can say is that sometimes, good people get caught up in the moment and make bad decisions. That's really all I can say."

Stacy didn't say a word, but maintained eye contact. Complete silence surrounded us, accompanied only by the sound of inhaling and exhaling. Stacy's fierce eyes said more to me than any words could have ever conveyed. I knew that she demanded a better explanation, so I continued speaking after taking a long, deep breath and a deliberate swallow.

"Maybe this relationship between us just happened too quickly. I mean, you just got out of your engagement and jumped right into another relationship. And maybe I felt a little pressured into the deal as well. I don't know, maybe we just moved too fast. I can't say that I was really ready for this."

She took a deep breath while shaking her head in frustration. Finally, unable to allow herself to continue listening to my excuses, she went completely the fuck off, screaming at the top of her lungs.

"Don't know if you're ready for this? DON'T KNOW IF YOU'RE READY? Are you fucking serious? Did you know you might not have been ready all those times you were FUCKING ME CAMERON? HUH NIGGA? DID YOU KNOW THEN? DID YOU KNOW THAT WHEN YOU WERE ALL UP IN MY DADDY'S FACE, KISSING HIS ASS?"

Her outbreaks of frustration continued for a few minutes, and when she finally calmed down, I offered an apology, which only seemed to upset her more. I reached for her hand, but she snatched away briskly.

"Don't touch me. Don't you dare fucking touch me Cameron," – she said to me in a relatively soft, yet angry voice.

By this time, the clock on her dresser displayed bold flashing numbers reading 2:27 a.m. I was tired, frustrated, and still afraid to fall asleep, so I made an attempt to leave.

"Stacy, I think I'll leave now."

"No Cameron, you ain't going no fuckin' where until I get back. You got me blocked in, so you can either take me to the store or you can move your freakin' car out of the driveway. "Just take my car," I suggested to her while tossing her my keys. I needed at least a little time to clear my mind, so I was somewhat anxious for her to leave, and I really didn't care where she was headed. I really just wanted to rest my head for a while, and I knew that this wasn't going to happen while she was there.

The combination of reckless curiosity and an effort to show concern prompted me to ask her where she was headed.

"Where you going at damn near three o'clock in the morning?" I asked with a concerned look on my face.

She responded with words that may have been even more devastating than any of tonight's events. In fact, I think I'd rather she had found a dozen video tapes rather than to hear her recite what came next. Still in an angry tone, she again lashed out.

"I'm going to the store to get a pregnancy test. I haven't had a period in three months Cameron."

Hearing this made me sick to my stomach. I would've just assumed to had fallen asleep and had her dowse me in hot grits than to deal with being the father of her child. I looked at Stacy in a manner which I'm sure resembled a fish on a hook or a deer in headlights. Still, I somehow mustered up the energy to speak.

"For real? Why are you just now telling me this?"

Still frustrated, she responded to my statement with frustration and anger in her voice.

"Cameron, fuck you. You wouldn't give a fuck either way. The only thing you care about is you Cameron. You can really save all the fake shit!! And I just want you to know that if I am pregnant, you're gonna' have to start being a little less selfish, cause I'm keeping my baby nigga." She continued lashing out, expressing her disappointment; exposing my selfishness; and criticizing my various character flaws. After a few minutes of this, she briskly walked out of the house, letting me know that she'd be back in 20 minutes.

The sound of the front door being slammed was immediately followed by the sounds of her starting my car and driving off into the distance. By this time, I was so outdone that I couldn't do much of anything other than stare aimlessly into space, as my own disturbing thoughts were the only thing keeping me company in her cold and empty home.

Of all of the events that took place on that dreadful day, nothing could have been worse than the possibility of Stacy being pregnant. At least that's what I thought. Little did I know, things were about to become even more dreadful.

For 45 minutes or so, I sat on pins and needles, impatiently awaiting Stacy's return with the pregnancy test. Another half an hour passed and she was still nowhere in sight. The keys to her SUV were sitting on the coffee table in the living room, so I grabbed my cell phone and took off in her car, hoping to find her. After about 25 minutes of driving and several unsuccessful attempts to call her, my cell phone finally rang with Stacy's number showing on caller-id.

"Damn Stacy. How long does it take to buy a pregnancy test?"

To my surprise, rather than Stacy's voice, the voice of a middle-aged white man responded on the other line.

"This is detective Bray, Wichita Police Department. Whom am I speaking with?"

At this point, I got slightly insecure, while considering that this may be some love interest of hers playing on the phone. I sat silently on the phone, until the sound of the officer's brisk voice continued speaking.

"HELLO. Are you still there? Detective Bray speaking."

By then, I was utterly confused, but just in case this was legit, I decided I had better cooperate, so I introduced myself on the phone.

"This is Cameron Banks, how can I assist you?"

Detective Bray responded with a question. "Mr. Banks, are you the owner of a black seven series BMW?" The officer went on to confirm my license plate number.

"Yes I am, is everything okay?"

"Mr. Banks, are you an associate of Stacy Underhill?"

By this time, I was borderline paranoid. Why is a police officer calling me from Stacy's phone? Why was he asking about my BMW? Nonetheless, I answered his question.

"Yes, she's an acquaintance of mine. Is everything okay?"

Detective Bray cleared his throat before answering; then requested that I come see him at the Northwest police substation. I rushed to the police station, which was only five minutes away, and went immediately inside to visit with the detective, eager to pacify my reckless curiosity.

Maybe it was just my imagination or perhaps it's just television, but like most black men, my perception is that anytime police officers deal with black men, the standard procedure is to use a crazy, hollering and yelling, ass kickin' white dude to come in with the 'scare-a-nigga' tactic. Then, in comes the cool, levelheaded black dude to balance off the intimidation with some good ole' fashioned black on black trust. In the back of my mind, I was wondering if this was what I had in store for me. In actuality, things transpired much differently than what I had expected.

Although a black detective named Officer Walker was there to assist Bray, and although Officer Bray couldn't have been more of a redneck even if his name was Bo, Luke, or Uncle Jessie; the meeting wasn't about interrogating me. The two officers took me into a comfortable conference room and informed me that my automobile had been involved in a shooting. They had apparently run the license plates on my BMW and examined Stacy's phone and seen the multiple calls I had made to her.

By that time, I was a frantic and nervous wreck. I wasn't sure what the angle of the officers was just yet, but I didn't care. All that concerned me at that moment was the well being of Stacy. I had always professed to have never loved her, but I was immensely bothered by the thought that she may had been in trouble. I also thought about the way that this incident would make me look in the eyes of Mr. Underhill and everyone else at the firm. I blurted out in the middle of the conversation.

"Where is Stacy? Is she alright? Where is she? I need to see her now."

The detectives calmed me down and assured me that I wasn't a suspect. I guess they just wanted to see if I knew anything that would help them with the case. Since Stacy was driving my car and I had obviously been trying to call her on the evening of the shooting, it wasn't out of the question to think that I'd be required to answer some questions.

The detectives gave me the information on where the situation had taken place, and immediately I had an idea as to what had happened. Stacy had discovered some type of clues that had led her to snoop in Cheyenne's neck of the woods. The crime scene was clear across town, less than a block from Cheyenne's house. After my conversation with the detectives was done, I debated between heading to the crime scene or the hospital. Assuming that Mr. Underhill would be at the hospital and a bit leery to face him, I rushed to the taped off crime scene first. The vehicle was pathetic. On the driver's side, there were at least five 9-millimeter bullet holes, plus the front windshield had also been shot out. I identified myself and asked one of the officers if I could take my personal belongings out of the vehicle that wouldn't be needed for the investigation. I was informed that this wouldn't be allowed, but from a distance, I could see the pregnancy test that Stacy had purchased sitting on the dashboard.

As if the shooting, the videotape, and the possible pregnancy weren't enough things to keep me stressed, I must also mention that my insurance on the BMW and all of my other vehicles had been lapsed for nearly four months now. In an attempt to catch up on some other bills, I had foolishly let my insurance expire, and the burden of coming up with the money to get the car fixed now added to my list of hardships. Not to mention, that in Kansas it is a criminal offense to be without automobile insurance.

From the outside looking in, I'm sure I looked about as fly as they come. In reality, my lavish lifestyle had caught up with me and I was slowly slipping behind the financial 8-ball. I didn't spend much time stressing over my own transgressions though. At that particular moment, my own personal issues weren't as important to me as Stacy.

I was certain that K-9 saw the car lurking around Cheyenne's house, made an assumption that it was me and unloaded on the vehicle. Without a doubt, I knew that this was what had happened, but I didn't have a clue how to handle the situation. Behind the suit and tie, I'm still from the hood, so calling the police wasn't even part of the equation. Besides, how would I sound explaining that my girlfriend was shot by my other girlfriend's boyfriend?

I rushed from the crime scene to the hospital, all while sickened in the stomach by the incident at hand. By now, the time was 3:52 a.m., and I parked Stacy's vehicle in a handicap stall and rushed inside the hospital's emergency area.

Mr. and Mrs. Underhill, their pastor, and a small group of their church members congregated in the emergency area, while all were impatiently awaiting the outcome of Stacy's condition. I wasn't surprised that Stacy's grandmother wasn't there. She had recently been experiencing heart problems, and the Underhill's most likely didn't want to stress her out with this incident.

As I entered the hallway of the emergency area, most of Stacy's friends and family greeted me warmly, with the exception of Mr. Underhill. I hugged Mrs. Underhill and shook hands with their pastor, but when I reached for Mr. Underhill's hand, he chose to greet me with an evil grimace rather than an extended hand.

With a puzzled look on my face, I dropped my hand back to my side and walked down the hallway until reaching a set of bench styled seats. I sat down to collect my thoughts, but shortly thereafter, Mr. Underhill approached and took a seat beside me.

In a sincere yet nonchalant tone, I said, "Hey Mr. Underhill."

Never acknowledging my cordial remark, Mr. Underhill began immediately lashing into me, but in an angry whisper so as not to disturb the relatively quiet hospital. With his forehead wrinkled and his voice shaking angrily, he said, "look here Cameron, this shit doesn't look right to me. You need to tell me what the fuck is going on."

"I'm not certain that I know what you mean sir?"

Still angry and with his eyes beginning to redden and water, Underhill said, "Oh yeah boy, you know what the fuck I mean."

I paused, took a deep breath, and searched unsuccessfully for words to possibly pacify the uncomfortable vibe that existed between the two of us. Just as I was about to open my mouth, he spoke up again.

"Look here you son of a bitch you! If I find out that you had anything to do with this shit. Anything at all to do with this, so help me God, I'll kill you."

My father taught me at a young age to always make direct eye contact in order to demonstrate my inability to be intimidated by other men. On this particular occasion, this practice didn't seem to work with Mr. Underhill. Though our eyes were connected and our expressions stale, I was already on Underhill's shit list and terrified to death at the thought of further fueling this. Still, I somehow mustered up the nerve to challenge him. In a voice that was both sincere and flustered, I spoke directly to Mr. Underhill.

"Look here Mr. Underhill, I know we may have had a conversation the other day about some of my actions, and yeah, I admit... I lied about some things I shouldn't have lied about. I admit, I fucked up, so if I'm a worthless piece of shit for lying, then so be it; I'll be that. But dammit, I do care about your daughter and I'd never put her in a situation that would harm her! Lying about why I was late for a meeting is one thing, so hold me accountable for that, but this... this is something different."

Mr. Underhill maintained the frown on his face, but seemed to buy in to what I had said. Still looking at me and remaining silent, he seemed to quietly demand that I continue explaining, so I did.

"Mr. Underhill, I know how you feel about Stacy, but I love her too. I swear to God, I didn't have anything to do with this."

The two of us continued sitting beside one another, but all conversation between us stopped. Everything that happened from that point on was slightly blurry to me. Typically I remember details, like the clothes people wear or the side conversations that take place. Strangely enough, I don't remember much about that moment, other than the image of Mr. Underhill, kneeling forward and hunched over, crying with his face in his hands.

If I got up and left, I'd be an asshole and if I tried to console him, I'd be an asshole. There was nothing for me to do except sit there uncomfortably and say nothing. I hoped for anything to interrupt this intense and very odd moment, but the strange silence remained for nearly twenty minutes.

Finally, Mr. Underhill stood up, wiped his eyes, and recommended that the two of us return to the area where the family was awaiting Stacy's outcome. He never acknowledged one way or the other whether or not I was in his good graces or on his shit list. Maybe he was still trying to decipher everything..

My mind's reckless wandering came to a halt when the doctor entered the room to update us on Stacy. I can't even remember the physician's name. All I remember was a small framed, middle-eastern man in blue scrubs speaking to Mr. and Mrs. Underhill with a heavy accent. Two of the bullets had hit Stacy. She had been shot once in the abdomen and once in the shoulder. She was listed in critical condition, and she wasn't able to breathe on her own. She also had severe cuts on her forehead and beneath her eye from the shattered windshield glass.

Whether Stacy would live or die was still a mystery. There was also still some question as to whether or not she would be paralyzed if she were to survive the bullet wounds. The only thing that wasn't a mystery at that point was whether or not Stacy was pregnant. The doctor informed us that Stacy was indeed pregnant, and that the bullet to the abdomen ended the pregnancy. I wasn't the least bit surprised that she was pregnant; in fact, I'd have been more surprised if she wasn't. The two of us had been freely engaging in unprotected sex during the entirety of our relationship, and Stacy wasn't using any type of birth control.

Originally, I was totally against Stacy having a child by me, and I probably would've even been so evil as to wish for her to lose the baby. However, I'd never be so sinister as to wish for her to lose her child in a manner of violence such as this. I remember truly hating myself at the moment we had received the news from the doctor. Though I had typically never owned up to much or accepted accountability for many things in the past, I realized that this was totally my fault and I couldn't have felt worse.

The reality of my own disturbing thoughts eventually had me so bothered that I could no longer sit around the Underhill's without feeling sick in the stomach. I knew what had happened, and like the worse piece of scum occupying the earth, I was sitting around the family pretending to be just as perplexed by this as everyone else. I couldn't take it any longer, so I cordially left everyone with hugs and handshakes and I excused myself from the hospital.

When I had gotten to the parking lot, my eyes were beginning to water just slightly. I opened the door, got in the car, and turned the key in the ignition. By the time I had pulled out into traffic, countless tears rolled down my face as I headed towards my home. I wasn't 100% sure exactly why I was crying. Maybe it was that I was disgusted with myself or maybe I was really concerned about Stacy. Regardless of the reason, I welcomed each tear. I was miserable, distraught, and lonely and my own teardrops seemed to be the only thing to keep me company. Perhaps this sounds a bit ridiculous, but at that moment, these very tears seemed to be the only element that I could confide in.

CHAPTER NINETEEN
Bitter November Rain

Back in the day, Baby Face and The Deele had a hit record called "Sweet November." Typically, I agree that November is a fun, festive, and even a sweet time of the year. Sweet dreams, sweet times, and sweet potato pie typically accompany the month in which Thanksgiving takes place. For me though, November would prove to be a very bitter and disturbing month. This would be the month that many of my lies and poor choices would finally get the best of me.

Stacy was in the hospital, and throughout most of the month, her condition hadn't improved much. As of Thursday, November 11th, she was still in critical condition and incapable of breathing on her own. Though she wasn't in a coma, her consciousness was limited and she still hadn't been able to talk. There was a strong chance that she wouldn't make it, and if she were to make it, there was a very strong possibility that she'd be paralyzed for life or extremely crippled. It was pretty much a given that if she were to make it, she would most likely be incapable of taking care of herself. I found it quite odd seeing her hooked to machines, unable to breath or use the restroom on her own - lying totally helpless. Everyday I would leave work early so that I could rush to the hospital to see her and be gone before Mr. Underhill would arrive. I knew that her condition was partially connected to some of the decisions I had made, and I just couldn't face being in the same room with her father. Especially since she wouldn't have even been in this circumstance had it not been for my selfishness and foolishness. I may have had no real compassion for Stacy as far as our intimate relationship goes, but I'm not a cold hearted and heartless person, and I did have a genuine concern for her as a human being.

This situation was killing me inside. Most of my visits consisted of me standing over her hospital bed, watching her and tasting each of my own bitter tears as they ran rapidly down both sides of my face and into the corners of my mouth.

Other poor choices and selfish decisions I had made were also catching up with me. I mentioned before that I didn't have insurance when the car was shot, and now I was being sued for the $38,000 I owed on the totaled BMW. Had the bank not known about the shooting, I would've been able to just continue making the monthly payments as though I was still driving the vehicle. Somehow the bank had discovered that the car was totaled though, and they were demanding the full balance immediately. My homeowners insurance, as well as the insurance on the other cars had also been cancelled for non-payment. I was so far extended financially and in such great debt, that I was having a hard time getting everything paid each month. My credit cards were maxed out from the purchase of items such as Rolex Watches, diamond earrings, at least 25 pair of Italian made shoes and various other luxuries. Also take into account that the BMW, the Jaguar, and the Escalade were all fairly new vehicles. Hell, I had $2400 per month going out in car payments alone, another $1300 just to make the minimum payment on all of my credit cards and roughly $1600 per month between student loans and other miscellaneous personal loans. Add these expenses with my $1875.58 mortgage payment, and combined, just these few bills alone equated to over $86,000 annually. Keep in mind that this didn't even include necessities such as groceries, gas, and utilities.

When it rains it pours. I distinctly remember adding all of these expenses in my head while crying beside Stacy's bed on the 11th, and thinking that things couldn't possibly get any worse. Then, on the way home from the hospital, Cheyenne called me for the first time since the encounter with her and K-9 back in September. I answered the call with the intention of talking shit. She had busted me in the head with a bottle, and I was almost certain that her worthless boyfriend had shot Stacy in an attempt to shoot me. I started to just ignore her call altogether, but I needed to get some things off my chest, so in a harsh and rude voice, I answered.

"What the fuck do you want?"

"God, do you have to be so rude?"

"If you don't want shit, I need to let you go Cheyenne. Bye."

"Wait, don't hang up. We need to talk."

"About what? About the cut you put on my fucking head? About your little trigger-happy ass nigga? What the fuck do we possibly need to discuss bitch?"

"Look Cameron, I didn't call to argue with you. I know you probably feel like I'm the biggest piece of shit in the world, and maybe I am."

"You said it bitch, not me!"

At this point in the conversation, her argumentative vocal tone had changed and I could hear sadness and disappointment in her voice. In fact, it appeared that she might have been crying.

"Alright fine, I'll be that. But I didn't call for that. I called because I really need your help."

Still cold and short, I replied, "Get that nigga to help you. Hell, you act like you can't breathe without this nigga. What the fuck? Is the nigga's dick must made out of cinnamon toast and saltwater taffy?"

"No Cameron. Please don't do this. Please."

"Hell, you can't seem to keep it out your mouth, so it must taste like something sweet. Is the mutha fucka coated in chocolate and peanut butter?" By then, I had started to amuse myself and I continued talking, with laughter in my voice, and with no intention other than to mentally tear Cheyenne apart.

"Yeah, that's it, ain't it bitch? Peanut butter and chocolate! Nigga got a Reese's Pieces dick, huh? Old Reese's Pieces dick having ass nigga, huh bitch?"

Aware that I had no intention of backing off, Cheyenne abruptly blurted out the words she had initially intended to say in the first place.

"Dammit Cameron, I'm four months pregnant."

I knew where this was going, and my stomach dropped to the floor. I immediately stopped fussing, and in a solemn voice, I replied, "Huh?"

"I didn't know how to tell you this with all the drama and everything, but I'm pregnant."

"So then I guess congratulations are in order for you and K-9? Make sure I get a cigar."

"Cameron, this isn't a joke. I'm pregnant and you want to crack jokes about the situation."

"I know you ain't trying to say that you pregnant by me are you?"

"That's just it Cam, I don't know. There's a possibility that the baby may be yours, and I can't take that chance. If that child comes out looking like you…"

"What… cute? Cause God knows that ugly ass nigga can't produce a cute child."

"Cameron, quit interrupting me. I don't have the money and I need help paying for an abortion."

"Why can't K-9 pay for the abortion? Hell, I'm broke."

"I asked him to pay for it."

"What he say?"

"He called me a ho, accused me of fucking around with you, and offered kicking me down a flight of stairs as his best solution."

Thinking to myself that this indeed could be my child that Cheyenne was carrying, and knowing that I couldn't afford to take care of a kid; nor could I afford to stay in the middle of all of the chaos surrounding her and K-9, I agreed to pay for the abortion.

"Cheyenne, I'll pay for the abortion, but you at least got an idea who the daddy is. Be honest, who do you think it is?"

"I think its K-9, but I'm not 100%. I just don't want to take any chances. Can you help me or not?"

"Oh, I'm definitely paying. I'm the one that can't take any chances. If there's even a 2% chance that I'm the daddy, I'm paying."

"I already made the appointment for November 29th at 9:00 a.m. That's the Monday after Thanksgiving."

"Cool, I'll make sure you have the money before then."

"Actually, I was hoping you could take me."

"Aw hell naw! I ain't sitting up in no fuckin' abortion clinic all day. Get your brother to take you. Hell, Jamal ain't got shit to do."

The two of us went back and forth for a while, before I finally agreed to take off to spend Monday the 29th with Cheyenne at the abortion clinic.

She went on to inform me that her process would take two days since she was already in her 2nd trimester. Typically, if an abortion is performed during the first six to eight weeks of pregnancy, the procedure is fairly simple. However, she was already at the point in which human form had begun developing. Therefore, she would be required to go through a process of being induced with drugs to stop the child's heartbeat on day one, and on day two having the fetus removed and destroyed. At the time, I believe that Kansas was the only state in the country that performed 2nd and even 3rd trimester abortions, and to me the process sounded brutal and downright nasty. Nonetheless, I knew I didn't want to father a child by Cheyenne, so I agreed to take off all day Monday so that I could drive her to the clinic, then to a nearby hotel. The clinic requires that all 2nd and 3rd trimester patients stay in this particular facility when enduring a two-day procedure. The second day, I would pick Cheyenne up from the hotel, take her back to the clinic, and when the procedure was complete, I would take her home. I definitely wasn't looking forward to this experience, but I realized that it needed to be done.

Exactly two weeks passed, and on Thursday, November 25th, I was pondering many things while driving to my parent's house on Thanksgiving Day.

Kansas is particularly beautiful during this season. Multiple shades of amber and brown leaves paint majestic abstract tapestries upon the earth's surface, and squirrels gathering acorns seem as surreal as animated figures in cartoons. During autumn days, radiant orange and blinding crimson sunlight spills across the sky like vibrant and fluorescent watercolors. The nighttime weather is usually accompanied by a soothing breeze and the peaceful sound of nature, and the stars seem so distant that constellations such as the winged horse Pegasus appear to have bodies molded of sculpted clay and polished moonlight.

    I had arrived late, so by the time I got there, a large group of family members were already feasting. I love good food and I do enjoy my family, so I should've been in good spirits. Lance called collect from prison to wish everyone a Happy Thanksgiving, and a host of cousins, aunts, and uncles seemed to all be actively engaged in eating entirely too much food while enjoying one another's company. With the exception of my grandmother, no one else seemed to realize that my heart was troubled. She kept asking me repeatedly if I was okay, and I would politely smile and answer, "Yes ma'am, everything is fine."

In actuality, I was far from being fine. Even in the company of great food and a wonderful family, my ability to enjoy the moment was tremendously hindered. A host of personal troubles were dominating the confines of my mental well being, sanity, and my very life itself.

After Thanksgiving dinner, it had become a tradition for us, and most other black families in Wichita, to watch the NFL doubleheader that Dallas and Detroit host against two opposing teams every Thanksgiving. Since we don't have a professional sports franchise anywhere in Kansas, you'll find that most of the locals are either Chiefs fans or Cowboys fans. Kansas City is only a 2 ½ hour drive from Wichita, and Dallas is approximately five hours, so it's not too hard to get to either place. The Detroit game is popular due largely to the fact that Barry Sanders is from Wichita. Although he did retire from the league in '99, lots of people from around here still cheer for Detroit simply because they either know Barry or they've seen him around town. Personally, I've never met or seen the guy, but I don't know if even he could've helped the Lions that day, as they played host to the Indianapolis Colts. The final score was 41-9 in favor of the Colts. I can't remember who Dallas played, or whether or not they won.

After watching the two games, we laughed and talked a while longer, then at around 8:00 p.m., everyone dispersed and headed back towards their respective homes. After helping mom clean up and wash dishes, I left at 9:45. By the time I got home, it was ten o'clock and I was mentally drained. I went inside the house; poured myself a glass of cognac with a twist of lime, consumed the drink, and went to bed.

On Monday morning, I woke up early so that I could call in to work, get dressed, and get Cheyenne to the abortion clinic in time for her appointment. By 7:00 a.m., I had showered and gotten dressed. At 8:00 a.m., I arrived at her house. She was dressed in a gray Nike sweat suit, a pair of white Nike's, and a gray baseball cap. She handed me her bag, which contained her overnight items, and we headed towards the car. I walked to the passenger side and opened her door, then got back into the Jaguar and headed towards the clinic. I was starving and wanted badly to stop and get a bite to eat, but I didn't want to eat in front of Cheyenne, who was put on what's called NPO (nothing per oral) by the doctor.

At around 8:15 a.m., we were attempting to pull into the driveway of the clinic, but several abortion protesters were blocking the driveway and marching with anti-abortion signs. Since Kansas is about the only place where abortions are performed on patients past eight weeks of pregnancy, there always seemed to be quite a bit of controversy with regards to abortions. I'd never been to the clinic before, so I wasn't sure what to expect, but I couldn't imagine us picking a worse day to have this procedure done. The receptionist later informed us that the clinic typically wasn't quite that hectic. She continued speaking, giving me some history that I could've lived without, but I listened intently as she explained that their most hectic time is in January. I guess January is the anniversary date of the landmark

Roe vs. Wade abortion case. I later discovered that this particular day's commotion was the result of a recent court decision to revisit the Roe v. Wade case or something... Fuck if I knew, I just wanted to get this nightmare over with.

    Local police officers, news media personnel, and protesters gathered to create so much commotion that all attempts of being discreet were thrown down the drain. The last thing I needed was for my car to be seen on television, unable to get to the abortion clinic due to protesters lying on the pavement and blocking the entrance. I had typically never taken one side or the other on the whole pro-choice or pro-life issue, but today I wasn't either... I was 100% pro-abortion. Protestors could've continued lying in front of my car if they wanted to, but one way or another, I was getting her ass in that clinic.

    By 8:45 a.m., the police officers had taken several protestors to jail and had managed to run off several others, so we were able to finally pull into the gated parking lot, where the fence was closed and locked behind us. By nine o'clock, Cheyenne and a small group of other women left the lobby to go and watch a short film, while I waited in the lobby with several of the other designated drivers. We were informed that the first day would take roughly six hours, and that the driver wouldn't be allowed to leave and come back later. Therefore, I would be stuck there all morning and all afternoon. What an exciting way to spend Monday morning - I thought to myself. I'm sure Janie was missing me, since I typically tried not to miss a Monday morning appointment. She may have even let old Theo get some since I was unavailable.

I brought a good book to read, so I figured I'd go ahead and start passing time. I opened the book and began reading, and after about 15 minutes had passed, a nurse in a white medical coat was escorting a teary eyed Cheyenne back into the lobby. The nurse spoke first.

"Mr. Banks, the young lady has decided not to go through with the procedure. I'm going to let you two discuss this in private."

The nurse led us to a small private room, where we talked for several minutes. I even tried my best to convince her that the abortion was the absolute right thing to do, but she just continued crying and repeating the same words continuously.

"I just can't do it Cameron. I can't do it. I'm sorry to put you through this, I just can't do it."

She then leaned her head on my shoulder and it remained there for the next couple of minutes until she had finished crying, and wiped her eyes with her index finger and thumb. By 10:00 a.m., we had left the clinic and by 10:15 a.m., I was pulling into her driveway. We sat in the car and talked for a while; she then kissed me on the cheek and told me thanks for everything. I drove away slowly trying to digest all that had just taken place.

Still dizzy from all of life's recent events, I decided that rather than going on to work, I'd take some time to get my thoughts together. Janie called me like she does most every Monday, but I really wasn't feeling that situation any longer. I couldn't continue to allow myself to be controlled by lust and all of my various other dysfunctions and shortcomings. Something would have to give, and that something was the irresponsible, childish, and selfish way in which I chose to approach life and relationships. Though I'd been to college, passed the CPA exam on the first attempt, established a successful career and traveled abroad, I still had yet to experience becoming a man. Sure my 31 years represented manhood from a legal perspective, but I realized at that moment that I still had yet to grow up. Prior to then, I guess I was too caught up in my own vanity and bullshit to realize this.

When I arrived home from Cheyenne's, I went to the bathroom to wash my face. After rinsing away the soap, I looked in the mirror at my dampened face and was truly disgusted with the person staring me eye to eye. It seemed that the mirror's reflection possessed most of the characteristics that had often disgusted me about others. I've often been told that the worst type of fool is one who sees a genius when looking in the mirror. Previously, I had been such a fool, but now for the first time - I saw the real me. I stood still – frozen in utter disgusted, as I exchanged cold stares, and eye to eye gazes with a liar, a cheater, a procrastinator, and a person who had created a vicious cycle of deceit, and games that had caused harm to everyone. Indeed, I seemed to be staring in the face of a true sociopath.

CHAPTER TWENTY
The Apprentice

On Wednesday, December 8th, I arrived at the office at 8: a.m. I needed to start getting busy and making money again, so that I could clean up my finances and get my life back on track. By 8:20 a.m., Mr. Underhill had already called me to his office. I didn't think much of it. I just figured he had an assignment he needed my help with. When I walked into the office, Mr. Underhill and his partner, Shelton Crabtree, greeted me. Also present were Mr. Wilkens, the HR Manager Brandy, and the head of security for our firm, Big Bruce.

I walked into the office, where everyone except Bruce was seated around Mr. Underhill's desk. Bruce closed the door behind me, and requested that I take a seat. He then positioned himself standing behind me, as Mr. Underhill began to speak.

"Cameron, you're probably wondering why I called you here, so I'll get straight to the point son."

I took a look around the room and noticed that all of the facial expressions were serious and stern. I'd never previously been in a meeting in which Bruce and Brandy were present, so I was beginning to get a bit worried, but I kept my composure and continued while listening to Mr. Underhill.

"Cameron, I've highlighted some items on a report you created for Mr. Wilkens. I want you to take a look at this and tell me what you think about it."

Mr. Underhill slid the multi-paged document across the desk, already flipped over to the page containing the highlighted information.

"Do you recognize any of this, son?"

I remained silent for several seconds, contemplating what to say. I finally decided to do something that I hadn't done for quite some time. I told the truth.

"Yes sir, I recognize exactly what's wrong with this report."

My little secret had been uncovered. The company being bought by Wilkens wasn't as financially sound as I had presented them to be, and although he would've still probably purchased them, my neglect was the reason for a gross overbid on his part, and the potential loss of a valuable client for our firm.

    Months ago, I had uncovered that the firm being purchased had disguised some of its expenses as capital expenditures. I won't go through the trouble of providing a lesson in basic accounting, but I will mention that this was similar to what had taken place with WorldCom. Long story short - capital expenditures are asset items that can be depreciated over a certain period, and expenses are debts that a business is currently liable for. When expenses are disguised as capital expenditures, the true expenses are listed as being lower than they actually are; thus, creating the illusion that an organization is more profitable than it truly is.

    Since I was occupied with activities such as sleeping with the client's daughter, along with various other acts of foolishness, I was embarrassed to report how late in the process I had detected this issue, so I intentionally overlooked it. I could've probably lied and pretended that I didn't catch it, but Underhill had worked with me long enough to know that this was one of the first things I usually look at with these types of ventures. Plus, some of the information on a few of my other reports had reflected clearly that I had detected this.

Mr. Underhill and Mr. Crabtree were obviously trying to save face with Mr. Wilkens and keep him as a client, and by now I had figured out that part of this plan was going to include firing me in front of Wilkens. What had given it away was the cardboard box sitting at the foot of Mr. Underhill's desk. I'd been in the corporate world long enough to know that once an employee is terminated; the company doesn't allow them back into the building. Security usually piles all of the employee's personal items into a box, and the employee is allowed to wait at the security desk for this process to be completed. Meanwhile, everyone in the office will most likely stare, whisper, and gossip about what may or may not had taken place. It's damn near like a soap opera.

Underhill gestured to Mr. Crabtree in case there was anything he wanted to add. Mr. Crabtree didn't offer anything, so Underhill continued speaking.

"Is there anything you feel like we need to hear, or anything you feel like saying?"

"No sir. I understand I dropped the ball on this, and I am okay with whatever disciplinary action you've opted to administer."

Realizing that this was both personal and business for Underhill, I can't say that I blamed him. Hell, I got his daughter shot, I made up an elaborate lie when I missed work, and he had accurately suspected that I was sleeping with Janie. Now I nearly cost him the most important account handled by his firm. I know he was about sick of my ass, but I commend him on remaining level headed and professional throughout the entire process. Then, with a slight smirk on his face, he calmly asked for my badge and my key to the building, and in a voice similar to that which Donald Trump uses on *The Apprentice*, he calmly looked me in the eye and said, "You're Fired. Brandy will visit with you briefly about unemployment benefits and how to roll your retirement plan into an IRA. Meanwhile, effective immediately, your employment with Wallace, Underhill & Crabtree is done." Underhill looked away from me and never again looked back in my direction. If he could've strangled me to death without being charged for it, there's no doubt in my mind he would've done just that.

Brandy spent about two minutes going over some paperwork with me then I was escorted to the front door by Bruce.

I left the office feeling as if I'd been kicked in the stomach and shit on. I was trapped in a serious financial bind, and I had just lost my only source of income. I had 'nickled' and 'dimed' my combined 401K and personal savings to just $6000, but I had over $7000 in bills due this month alone. Though I was eligible for unemployment, it only paid about $400 per week, which wasn't even enough to pay my minimum credit card bills, much less any significant bills like the mortgage or auto loans. The fact of the matter was that I was flat broke, and had no means of maintaining my lifestyle.

Hell, I couldn't even afford my basic day-to-day necessities.

Chapter Twenty-One
Hurt So Bad

All alone – On your own
You realize what you had
And you didn't know it hurt so bad

By December 22nd, I had decided to pack up my things and get out of Wichita. For two weeks straight, I had been actively seeking a job, but no one would even as much as talk to me. It was pretty clear that Mr. Underhill had whiteballed me in this town. He could've gone as far as reporting me and possibly causing me to lose my license, so I guess I do have something to be thankful for.

Rather than rolling my 401K, I cashed it out. I tried arranging with the bank to get the BMW paid off, but they refused to budge. I knew that I would eventually have to file for bankruptcy, but for now, I sent $2000 just to cover the past due, and to pacify them for a month or so. I took my remaining life savings of $4000 and paid on my house note, student loans and credit card bills. The Escalade was leased, so I took it back to the dealership. I figured they'd charge an early lease termination fee, and they did. I didn't have the money, so I made sure to save them a special place on my credit report, right along with special spots I would reserve for various other creditors.

Oddly enough, Theo Huxtable was interested in buying the Jaguar. Janie mentioned how much he liked it when I was visiting her one Monday, and on December 16th, he purchased it for about $3300 more than what I owed on it. I used $1300 towards the purchase of a rather raggedy ass '95 Ford Escort with a good motor, and used the remaining $2000 to help accommodate my move to Dallas, Texas. Meanwhile, I put my home on the market the same day that Underhill fired me, and since it was listed as a short-sale, I had an offer within 10 days. I accepted the offer on the 18th, and though I was selling the home well below its value, I had a contract and was scheduled to close near the middle of January.

On the morning of the 22nd, I headed down I-35, heading south for the peaceful five hour journey that would pass through Oklahoma City and end in the Dallas/Ft. Worth area. Since the car didn't have a radio or stereo that worked, I was able to do some serious soul searching during the trip.

I had spoken with Reggie, and told him about my situation. Reg was actually the person who suggested that I come to Dallas for a while and start all over. He did make it clear that two weeks was the maximum length of time that I'd be able to reside at his home, but hopefully I wouldn't need much longer than that..

With nothing to my name except an expensive wardrobe, a bucket Ford and $2000 cash, I was ready to seek out new territory. I lost the home, the job and the cars, and of course, the women disappeared soon after. I piled everything worth packing into the trunk and the backseat of the Ford Escort, and everything worth keeping for later was put into storage.

I stopped to visit Stacy at the hospital before I hit the highway. Her condition still hadn't gotten much better. In fact, she had reverted back to using the breathing machine. This was all my fault and I prayed to

God that if he would correct this for me, I'd never be so selfish again. Stacy had once said that the only person in life that I've ever cared about was myself. Though it bothered me to hear her say this, I realized how true this statement was as I looked down on her severely wounded body. Though she was only slightly conscious, and probably didn't even know I was there, I kissed her on the forehead and proceeded to leave. I was hoping that I wouldn't see Mr. Underhill at the hospital, but as I was leaving the room, I crossed paths with him and his wife. I felt awkward, but I still spoke.

"Good morning, Mr. and Mrs. Underhill."

Mr. Underhill walked by me as if he didn't notice me, and Mrs. Underhill gave a slight head nod, but didn't really acknowledge me either. It was a very uncomfortable situation for me, but I can't say that I didn't deserve this treatment.

I got in the car and finally got on the highway. I had to bundle up for the trip. When I bought the car, the heat worked, but now I couldn't get the vents to blow anything other than cold air. December is typically a cold month in Kansas, and this year was no different. By the time I left the hospital, the temperature was about 11 degrees, so the first few hours of driving were miserable. Fortunately, I was heading south and I'd already checked to see that the temperature in Texas was in the low to mid 60's.

Driving a cold car, down a cold highway, on a cold day in a cold world, I thought about all that I had left behind in Wichita just three days prior to Christmas. For starters, this would be the first Christmas that I'd ever spend without my family. Then there was Cheyenne who would have a baby in March, and I had to wait until then to find out whether or not I was the father. There was also Stacy, who was hospitalized and I could only hope for her to experience a full recovery. The guilt I felt from this situation was killing me. I had been back in brief contact with Cathy again, but I tried to avoid her whenever possible. Since I'd lost my job and cars, she'd somewhat lost interest anyway, just as I expected. I heard through the grapevine that Theo Huxtable and Janie were engaged to be married, and I honestly wished the best for them. Considering that she was trying to see me less than two weeks prior, I worried that Theo might be making a poor choice. Of course, I'm certainly not qualified to challenge anyone's choices. I just hoped that she wouldn't find herself attracted to someone who may just had happened to have some free time available on Monday's. If so, that marriage would be doomed from the start. The other thing I thought about was K-9. I wasn't sure what to do, but I knew I couldn't let him off the hook that easy. I was cool with fighting him one on one, but I wasn't too comfortable with the gangster element he added to the mix. I'd have plenty of time to sort everything out later. For the time being, I just needed to get settled, get a job, and get back on my feet..

  I arrived at Reggie's house at two-thirty in the afternoon and unpacked my things. Reggie was divorced and had two sons, both six years old. One of the boys was by his ex-wife, and the other by his ex-mistress. That's another story in itself that will be discussed later. For now, the boys were both gone to live in other states with their mothers. Reggie directed me to the boy's room, which had Spiderman bedspreads on both the bottom and top bunks, and matching Spiderman window curtains. Posters of Dragon Ball-Z and various other animated characters surrounded the parameter of what would become my home for the next two weeks. I took a long, deep breath and slowly exhaled, then thought to myself that this day would be the first day of the rest of my life. I had learned my lessons and I promised myself that I'd never go down this destructive path again.

EPILOGUE

They say that most everyone's life story is appealing enough to make for an interesting reality show. If I'd never believed that before, I certainly did after 2004. In fact, my life in '04 was like a mix-tape of reality show greatest hits, complete with some occasional movie clips edited in. By the end of the year, I'd had my choice of women like Flava Flav and I'd been physically attacked as if I were exposed on the *Jerry Springer Show*. I was even busted on videotape in a manner that the producers of "Cheaters" would've loved to broadcast. Hell, in between run ins with "Cops", I somehow found time to be fired as if I were the "Biggest Loser" on "The Apprentice". Other than "Making the Band", I'd just about done it all. I even found myself in movie situations similar to those of Denzel in "Out of Time" and Giovanni Ribisi in "Boiler Room." Indeed, my life was dramatic, dangerous, and chaotic, yet still truly entertaining. I imagine you're reading this passage and thinking the same about your own life, and laughing silently about all the things about you that the people in your life will never know. Be careful not to laugh too loudly though, because each of those individuals has a similar reality show playing itself out as well. As for me, I can truly say that my season has ended and my show is out of syndication. Hopefully you can say the same. Of course, even after the season is over, there are still repercussions that must be dealt with ... repercussions that stem from poor choices and reckless lifestyles...

Most men typically have good intentions going into relationships. Some of us even imagine ourselves walking down marriage aisles, purchasing dream homes, sending kids to college, and growing old with that special someone. At times we even imagine being faithful. Hell, for all I know... there may be a few faithful and happy couples still existing in this old crazy world. Regardless of whether or not faithfulness exists, I can certainly attest that love does. I can honestly say that in my own sick and distorted manner; other than Cathy, I had allowed myself to fall in love with everyone of the women in this story. In fact, there are a few others that I neglected to mention, and I must admit that I was in love with each of them as well.

Therefore, the absence of love isn't what I perceive to be the problem. In actuality, the problem is curiosity. The constant desire to chart and explore new territory seems to be the thirst that most men (and even some women) have trouble quenching. It seems as if our carnal desires are driven by the constant and never-ending appetite to seek and conquer that one particular and very special component of the female anatomy... That section of the feminine physique that is typically unseen in public places, yet its appearance, feel, smell, texture, and fabric are often imagined and visualized by curious spectators – familiar acquaintances and complete strangers alike... Indeed, I am referencing the part of the woman that doesn't assist with active tasks such as walking and talking; nor does it aid any of the seven senses in performing their specified operations – yet and still; it has caused families to separate, friendships to end, strong men to become weak, and powerful nations to crumble. It has no voice, yet in darkness, it whispers many languages... It has no heart, yet its pulse is vibrant and alive... Its' attraction is intense to the point that evokes lust and desire so robust that men have chased it, lied for it, stolen for it, purchased it with cash and expensive gifts, and even murdered because of it. Typical thesauruses have no alternate word choices for its politically correct scientific name, yet worldwide it is known by many appropriate, yet inappropriate pseudonyms. The songwriter Rick James referred to it as "that sweet, that nasty, funky stuff," and Prince - even more direct - when boldly proclaiming its power as something that he simply referred to as "Pussy Control." Monologues, chronicles, books, and even movies have been dedicated to this mysterious and desirable substance; and have identified it by a plethora of additional autographs and monograms. Perhaps none of these brands have encompassed its essence quite as well as Lauren Hill, when she vividly described it as "That Thing". Therefore, I must confess that it was indeed this very 'thing' that served as the center of all of my shortcomings and transgressions. Certainly some parts of this 'thing' are admirable, sweet, and precious.

However, each of these elements is met with a balanced portion of that which is unattractive, bitter, dangerous, and downright nasty. Indeed I seemed to have had it all, but I had allowed my pursuit of "That Thing" to take control over my life and nearly destroy me and others. I sure hoped that I had learned my lesson, but only time would tell how I would react when encountering "That Thing" again in the future. Whether I would make the same mistakes or not, only the future would tell. One thing was definitely for certain though… I wasn't the first, nor would I be the last man to fall victim to its powerful mystique and irresistible inducement. I wouldn't be the last to lose damn near everyTHING simply because of "THAT THANG"

BE SURE TO ORDER "THAT THANG"
by Kevin Harrison at bglobalentertaimnet.com
AVAILABLE MOTHERS DAY – 2012

CPSIA information can be obtained
at www.ICGtesting.com
Printed in the USA
LVHW110753260322
714397LV00028B/113

9 781424 336708